Down & Dirty: Zak

Dirty Angels MC®
Book 1

Jeanne St. James

Editor: Proofreading by the Page
Cover Artist: Golden Czermak at FuriousFotog
Photographer: CJC Photography
Cover Model: Gus Caleb Smyrnios

---

www.jeannestjames.com

Sign up for my newsletter for insider information, author news, and new releases:
www.jeannestjames.com/newslettersignup

Keep an eye on her website at http://www.jeannestjames.com/or sign up for her newsletter to learn about her upcoming releases: http://www.jeannestjames.com/newslettersignup

Author Links: Instagram * Facebook * Goodreads Author Page * Newsletter * Jeanne's Review & Book Crew * BookBub * TikTok * YouTube

Acknowledgments

A HUGE thank you to Judy and Kenny Vodila for answering all my questions when it came to MC's. You were an important part of this book!

And even though it's fictional (and a romance), I hope it's true to life as much as an MC romance can be.

Dedication

At an author takeover on Facebook, there was a "game" played where you had only $5.00 to spend on the characteristics you wanted in a lover/spouse/partner. I spent my $5 to pick the following characteristics on my ideal partner. I chose:

A cop
Tattoos
Funny
G-Spot Magician
Good with his Tongue

Afterward, I realized I hit the jackpot and I had all that. Thank you, baby, for being so supportive. Love you. (You know who you are.)

Author's Note

With the end of the Brothers in Blue Series, I was sad to let the Bryson family go. So, I was determined to create another "family" of sorts. This time only a couple of them are cops. The rest? Well, they are rough talking, tough acting, and ready to get "down and dirty" bikers. But in the end, these men will do anything for their women. And, to me, that's all that matters.

Welcome to Shadow Valley, Pennsylvania, where the Dirty Angels MC rules...

Chapter One

A HIGH-PITCHED BUZZ SOUNDED. The magnetic door latch released and with a violent push, Zak stepped out into the sunlight.

Not even six feet from the building, he stopped, closed his eyes, flared his nostrils and inhaled a deep breath.

Smelled like freedom.

He opened his eyes, spun on his heels and raised his arms to give the double middle finger salute to the guards watching him on the cameras. He threw his head back and laughed.

Fuck them all.

His breath condensed in the frigid air and he wore no jacket but he didn't care.

Life. Was. Good.

A horn honked and he turned to see who it was. Though, it wasn't who he'd hoped, he wouldn't gripe about it. A brother was a brother, whether blood or not.

He picked up the small bag of personal items from where he dropped it in his haste to flip the guards the bird and jogged to the curb where his chariot awaited.

Diesel tossed him his leather cut, as well as a hooded sweatshirt. After pulling the sweatshirt over his T, he raised his colors to his nose and inhaled.

Yeah. His vest smelled like leather, smoke, booze and pussy. Best combination in the world.

The patch was dirty and worn but still made a clear statement. He was a fucking Dirty Angel and after ten years in the joint, that still hadn't changed.

This was his homecoming. And it would be his last one because he swore to himself he would never go into that concrete box again.

Never.

Diesel, the club's Enforcer, wore a huge grin when they clasped hands and bumped chests. "Good to see you, brother."

The man's smile was infectious. "Same, brother. Been too fuckin' long." He jabbed a finger at the Sergeant at Arms patch on the man's cut. "See nothin's changed. Still bustin' heads?"

Diesel only grunted and moved around the hood of the car to the driver's side.

Zak yanked open the door of the classic Pontiac GTO—Diesel's baby after his bike—and slid onto the seat, holding his cut on his lap like it was precious. Before climbing in, Diesel shrugged out of his, turned it inside out and slipped it back over his shoulders.

You never wore your colors when riding in a "cage," and if you did, you turned your colors in. Because DAMC was a damn bike club, not a car club. That was a lesson not to be forgotten. Zak smiled at the memory of kicking a prospect's ass for disrespecting the club by wearing his vest colors out while in a car.

Good times.

As Diesel pulled away from the parking lot, the larger man's head swiveled to study him, but Zak wasn't in the mood to talk about his time inside so he said, "Let's get the fuck outta here."

"Sounds like a plan. Need to get to church anyway, everyone's gettin' together for your homecomin' celebration."

Zak glanced at him in surprise. "Yeah?"

"Fuck yeah. Want to welcome home our president."

Zak shook his head and frowned. "I'm no longer president, D. Even I'm aware of that."

Diesel grunted, then said, "That'll change," and turned the key.

The throaty roar of the big block engine was music to Zak's ears. He couldn't wait to get the power of his bike between his thighs again. He'd missed it.

He'd missed the open road.

He'd missed doing shit on his timetable and not the warden's.

Even so, he hadn't missed being the club president and didn't know if he even wanted the hassle anymore. He wanted to enjoy his newly found freedom for a while. And being constantly saddled with club business choked that freedom.

But as his gaze slid to Diesel, he didn't think the time was right to talk about it.

They had a party to go to.

Beer to drink.

He needed to reconnect with his brothers.

And, almost as important, he needed to fuck some pussy. Because ten years was way too long to go without.

First order of business back at the club was to make his rounds. Second was to drain his clogged pipes.

And if it took more than one woman to do it? So be it.

When Diesel pulled the GTO through the gate into the rear parking lot of the clubhouse, a sense of relief overcame Zak. He breathed easier and felt himself automatically settling back into the old ways. He was home. Really fucking home.

He'd noticed there were no bikes or cars parked out front on the public side of the clubhouse, The Iron Horse Roadhouse. Hawk must have shut the bar down so everyone could attend the pig roast, which would be held out back, the private side of church.

"Got the girls to clean out one of the larger rooms upstairs so you got somewhere to crash tonight. Stay as long as you want. You know the deal."

Zak didn't answer, he only nodded, amazed at the sight of how packed the back lot was with vehicles.

Large fucking turnout.

Anxiety crept through him, his stomach churning a bit. He'd been gone a long time. A whole fucking decade. Things looked the same so far, but he knew there had been changes. Hopefully for the better.

Club life hadn't stood still waiting for Zak to do his time. His fingers fisted in his cut as it laid on his lap.

Diesel parked directly in front of the back entrance to the clubhouse—it was almost as if the spot had been reserved for him—and shut the car off, not moving to get out.

Zak didn't, either. Instead, he rolled his gaze up to read the sign over the gray steel-metal door.

Dirty Angels MC.

Under that, in smaller letters... *Down & Dirty 'til Dead.*

His nostrils flared as he sucked in oxygen.

This was his family. They would welcome him home with open arms.

Well, *they* would.

His dad and brother... not so much.

He mentally shook that problem out of his head and shot a look at Diesel before pushing the door open and unfolding from the passenger seat. As soon as he was on his feet, he shrugged his cut over his shoulders.

That was more like it. *Now* he was home.

He glanced down to where the rectangular patch was missing, where it had been ripped free from the leather, just a few stray threads left behind as a reminder.

He was no longer president. Someone else wore that patch now.

More power to Pierce for taking on the headache.

Though, some of the brothers weren't thrilled with Pierce taking the head of the table. Even though they were all brothers at heart, Pierce didn't come from either bloodline of the two club founders, Doc and Bear.

And Pierce didn't always agree with all of the club's business staying on the upside, staying legit. He tended to lean toward the old ways.

But the old ways had gotten way too many of them locked up. And when a brother was doing time, that meant less money in the coffers. One less member paying dues, one less member working in the businesses.

And that was not good. Not good for the club in general. Not good for the brothers who remained on the outside because they had to step up to fill in the financial gaps.

"Gonna just stand there, or gonna take your ass inside?" Diesel prodded, making Zak shake himself mentally to get himself out of his head, his thoughts.

With a smile to his brother, he kissed the tips of his fingers then leapt straight up, tagging the club's entryway sign with his hand.

Good to be home.

Diesel grunted, yanked open the door, and shoved Zak past the threshold into the dim interior.

Then the sound was deafening. The hooting, the hollering, the cat calls, the whistles, and "fuck yeah's," as Zak parted the crowd like the Red Sea. The common area was packed. Familiar faces became a blur as he fought his way through the back pats, shoulder bumps, forearms clasps. His face began to ache from the smile he wore; it couldn't get any bigger, any wider.

He pushed his way to the club's private bar and stared at Hawk stationed behind it. The big man had his thick arms crossed over his chest and a serious expression on his face. He looked the same as Z remembered, just ten years older. A few lines at the corners of his dark brown eyes, his dark hair in a short mohawk. That hadn't changed, either. Both sides of his head were shaved, his bare scalp sporting tattoos.

His right-hand man.

Or used to be, anyway. Zak's gaze dropped to the man's rectangular patch and was pleased to see the man was still VP.

But Zak knew that. He had been kept up to date for the most part during his stint at the State Correctional Institution in Fayette county. Most of the brothers had taken turns visiting when they could. Not that Zak expected them to, but it was good when they did.

It took everything in his power not to leap over the bar and grab the man only two years his senior into a bear hug. No matter what shit went down, Hawk always had his back.

Through thick and thin. Maybe not true brothers, but brothers all the same.

"Still as ugly as ever, chicken hawk," Zak growled at him. "Bet your hair is stiffer than your dick ever gets."

"Give me limp dick just thinkin' 'bout how many salads you tossed in the joint."

Zak realized how quiet the room became around them. All eyes on them.

"What's a man gotta do to get a damn drink 'round here?"

Hawk grabbed his junk. "Suck my cock. Probably good at doin' that now. Probably a pro."

"Fucker," Zak grumbled, struggling to keep a straight face.

Izzy walked behind the bar and in between the two men having a stare down. "Boys. Just kiss and get it over with. And then get the man a damn drink."

Zak's eyes slid to Isabella. "Damn, Izzy, you're lookin' good."

"Anything with a pussy probably looks good to you right now. But," she put both palms on the bar and leaned toward Zak, "it helped that I got rid of that rat bastard." She slapped a shot glass in front of him and cocked an eyebrow.

"Jack."

Izzy nodded then turned to grab the Jack Daniels from the shelf behind the bar. "Call me Bella, Z. I'm trying to erase anything that reminds me of him." She poured him a double.

He raised the glass up to her in a salute. "Here's to freedom. For both of us." Then downed the whiskey. The burn down his throat felt good. Real. A reminder that he was now free and needed to keep it that way.

"Amen to that," she muttered.

But she did look good. Her wavy, long dark brown hair went past the middle of her back. Her dark brown eyes looked guarded, as they should with the shit she went through with her former husband. Even though it was chilly out, she wore a tight black tank top with the letters DAMC over her ample breasts with her pink bra straps showing. A wide black leather belt cinched her narrow waist, and her hips... Damn, they'd widened out perfectly. Grab worthy, *hang on tight as she's bucking wild on your lap* worthy.

But even so, he wouldn't fuck her with a ten-foot pole. And one reason was standing directly behind her, watching him check her out. The other reason sidled up next to him. Diesel. Both men were brothers for real. And both men were her cousins who now kept a close eye on her. *Very* close. And he certainly didn't need a double ass-kicking fresh out of the joint.

"Know it's been ten years, but don't even think about it," Diesel muttered near his ear.

Zak lifted both palms in surrender. "Wouldn't even go there."

"Good."

They seemed to be more protective of her now than ever. And with good reason. He had heard what her ex had done to her. And he understood them getting their hackles up when a male showed interest. Though, she worked at The Iron Horse and he couldn't imagine she didn't get hit on a lot. Her curves had matured over the last ten years and he had to admit she was drop-dead gorgeous. He wondered how many asses Hawk and Diesel thumped because of that.

Izzy shifted down the bar to talk to someone else and Hawk stepped back up, pouring him another double then pouring one for Diesel and himself. They clinked shot glasses then downed them in one swallow.

Zak slapped the glass down on the bar top and got serious. "Anyone see my dad or Axel?"

He didn't miss when Diesel and Hawk's eyes met briefly, a silent message, then their gaze broke and went back to him.

"See 'em 'round town, but haven't had any real run-ins with 'em."

"Guess they won't be here tonight," Zak said softly, trying to fight the disappointment, but having a hard time keeping it from his voice.

"You know how it is with those fuckin' cops, Z," Jag said, walking up behind him and pounding him a welcome on the back. "They stick with their own. Don't wanna get dirt under their nails by fraternizin' with us."

Zak turned to his cousin, and they clasped hands as if they were about to arm wrestle and then bumped shoulders.

Jag muttered, "Fuck that," and wrapped his muscular arms around Zak and squeezed him tight.

Zak thought he spotted a tear in his blood relative and the club Road Captain's eye.

Nah. Couldn't have been.

Dirty Angels never cried. Even when they did.

And if they did, no one noticed or talked about it. Ever.

One time a prospect made fun of a patched member who got emotional and he ended up disappearing. Just like that.

Poof.

But then that was in the old days.

Even a hard-assed MC member shed some tears once in a while. But, again, somehow no one ever noticed.

"Uncle Mitch an' your brother have been scarce. When the pigs show up here, for whatever reason they feel's 'necessary,' they usually send anyone but them. An' from what I heard, they've circled the wagons 'round Jayde since she's come home from college. Don't want her gettin' anywhere near the club or any of us dirty fuckers."

"With good reason," Zak joked. Or tried to. He missed his little sister. The last time he saw her she was around fourteen years old. His mother and she had sat in the back of the courtroom for his sentencing and once it was over, he turned to look at them and they were gone. Disappeared. It probably had been too much for them.

So, he didn't blame them. And he tried not to take it to heart that no one from his immediate family had ever visited him once while he was at Fayette. He understood their desire to keep their lives separate.

Though, his grandfather would have been pissed if he'd still been alive. The club had been his grandfather's heart and soul.

Fuck.

He was supposed to be celebrating, not getting morose.

Zak cleared the thick out of his throat and said, "Proud of you for gettin' voted in as Road Captain."

Jag dropped his head, breaking eye contact, and murmured, "Nah, it was nothin'. Someone had to step up."

"Glad it was you."

Suddenly, he was body slammed from the back. Then slammed again. He turned to see Ace, Diesel and Hawk's father, and Dex, their cousin and Izzy's brother.

"Holy fuck, boy, you don't look worse for wear," Ace boomed. "C'mere, you fucker."

Ace pulled Zak into his arms and squeezed tight, making it hard for Z to breathe, but before he let go, he murmured in his ear, "Thank fuck you're out. Gotta get this club back on track."

Zak schooled the surprise from his face before he turned to Dex, who only smiled at him and said, "Fuckin' A, brother. You've been greatly missed."

Zak's lips thinned and he nodded. The back of his throat tickled with unshed tears and he blinked away any evidence of weakness.

To cover up his emotions, he pointed at Ace's patch which read Treasurer, and shouted, "You assholes still trust this guy with our money?"

Laughter surrounded him. Then he spun on Dex and pointed to his patch. "Secretary? Who taught Dex how to read an' write?"

Dex laughed, pounded him on the back and grabbed the shot glass Izzy shoved at him. He lifted it toward Zak in salute and then downed it.

Ace grabbed Zak's arm and pulled him over to the side, leaning in. "Left a message on your father's phone to let him know you were comin' home today." Ace shook his head, his face dropping. "Sorry, son. Didn't even get a text back."

"To be expected," Zak said, then gave him a reassuring half smile. "Thanks for tryin', though."

Then a booming voice rose from out of the crowd. "Get the fuck outta my way."

Grizz.

Goddamn. It was going to get even harder to hide his emotions once that old man got to him. The crowd of onlookers let him through and he stopped about five feet from Zak, inspecting him from head to toe.

"Don't look worse for wear," Grizz echoed Ace.

"Hell, no," Zak answered. "Was like Club Fed in there. Couldn't ask for a better vacation."

"Boy, come give this ol' man a bear hug." And with that, he opened his thick arms wide and Zak, with a smile, stepped into them. "Fuckin' A," Grizzly mumbled and sniffed.

"Don't you start," Zak warned softly. "You start an' I'm a goner."

Grizz nodded and then shoved Zak away from him. Zak caught his balance before facing the older man who was like a grandfather to him. Hell, like a grandfather to most of the members of the club. He'd been around forever. Zak couldn't remember this club without him. His beard was longer, bushier, and definitely grayer than the day Zak got locked up. But his light blue eyes twinkled. He was still as sharp as a tack.

"Ten years in the slammer, son. Earned your wings. I'll get my ol' lady to put 'em on your cut. An' get Crow to add 'em to your tats."

Zak nodded to avoid creating any drama, but he didn't want the wings. On his cut, on his body, or otherwise. He wasn't proud of being a convict. A felon.

A jailbird.

And he didn't need a permanent reminder of that, either. But he kept that to himself.

"Okay, enough of this fuckin' mushy homecoming. It's time to party like real men. Bonfire's rollin', pig's turnin', an' there's plenty of pussy for everyone. Even you, Z."

Zak turned toward the bar and saw Pierce, the current club president, standing on the polished surface, high above everyone crowded around it. A collective shout went up at his announcement and the crowd started filing out the side door to the courtyard where they had an outdoor pavilion, picnic tables, and all the shit they needed to party like a club should.

More people patted him on the back as they passed him. Some he knew. Some he didn't. Some wore cuts, and a few of the women wore them, too.

Ol' ladies.

He wondered how many of the members were now saddled with a ball and chain.

Fresh out of the box, he was going to make sure he didn't have any of the sweet butts or female hang-arounds dig her claws into him. When it was warm enough to drag his sled out, he wanted no one on the back clinging on to him. He had plenty of time for that later.

Now... Now, he was going to enjoy life.

But first, he was going to get shit-faced. Then get laid. Or vice versa.

Zak hooted loudly, then got swept outside with the rest of the crowd.

Chapter Two

ZAK SLIPPED into the deserted clubhouse. He needed a quick break, a little peace and quiet... from the band, from the brothers, from the prospects who were looking up to him—which they shouldn't. He decided to slip away and grab a drink inside. He'd been kept busy outside and hadn't had a chance to drink himself into oblivion yet.

Even worse, he hadn't found anyone yet to drag upstairs to his bed, either. He couldn't bang any of the women out there that he respected, like Izzy aka Bella, or Kelsea, or even Ivy. Even though they weren't related by blood, they were still his "sisters" since they were Doc's granddaughters. It just wouldn't feel right to bust a nut with them.

No. But so far, none of the female hang-arounds or sweet butts had caught his attention either.

He shouldn't be this picky. Not at all. Once he broke the seal on his ball sac, he hoped he would stop being so selective. But it'd been ten years, so for some reason, he didn't want the first time to be with just anyone.

Maybe after more beer and Jack, he would slide on the "beer goggles" and he just wouldn't care who it was anymore. Though, he would need to make sure he wore a wrap. Some of the females out there did anything wearing colors, even the prospects, who weren't even fully patched members yet.

No. He needed to get on the ball and grab someone. Literally.

Or he'd be stuck with the girls Dawg had lined up for him. He didn't really want paid pussy. Not if he could help it.

He spied the bottle of Jack Daniels that had been left behind on the bar from their shots earlier and beelined to it. With the twist of the cap, he ignored the shot glass and began to lift the bottle directly to his lips.

At least until the back door banged open, and a whirlwind swept in. The whirlwind's eyes immediately landed on him and she approached in a flash, her long dark hair wild, her green eyes wide.

"Shit! I'm sorry I'm late."

Hot fucking damn.

As soon as she got close enough, he grabbed her hand and yanked her even closer, snaking a hand around her hip, drawing a gasp from her.

His balls tightened at the sound and he looked her up and down. "Sure you were worth waitin' for."

She certainly was. Her thick, wavy hair fell over her shoulders and down her back, and her pink lips, made for wrapping around his cock, parted.

She tried to tug her hand out of his and shift away from his hip. He held on tighter. "If you'd just tell me where you want the cake set up—"

"They fuckin' have 'em jumpin' out of a cake? Damn."

She leaned as far away from him as she could and looked up into his face, a frown marring her perfection. "What?"

"The girls Dawg lined up for me. You all gonna be jumpin' out of a cake? Like naked?"

She shook her head, her cheeks suddenly full of color. "I—"

Which was really cute. Hell, *she* was really cute.

No. She was stunning. And fucking hot as hell. Not cute.

He found what he'd been searching for. She'd be perfect to start the night out with. If Dawg had more women like this and some of them wanted to join in later, he wouldn't complain.

He dropped his head and kissed her hard, sliding his hand off her hip to her sweet, curvy ass and squeezed.

Fuck, did she taste good, too. Sweet, like icing. He dipped his tongue between her lips and explored her mouth with the tip of his tongue.

She made a noise. A groan? Yeah, she liked it, too.

His fingers raked through her long hair to hold her head still as he deepened the kiss. Fuck, he could eat her whole right this minute.

Eat her mouth, eat her pussy, then fuck her until she couldn't move.

The strippers at the club must have improved over the years. He never remembered them ever looking this wholesome. This natural.

But it was a nice touch. He'd have to compliment Dawg on upping the quality.

When he broke the kiss, she blinked up at him in a daze, her mouth parted and breathing hard.

"I don't... I'm not..." she started, looking a bit confused. "I'm looking for—"

"You found what you're looking for. You must be new."

"Yes, I'm—"

"Me, too," Zak said, grabbing her wrist and dragging her behind him to the back stairway. "Let's get this party started."

Finally.

His cock had already started without him. It pressed painfully against the zipper of his jeans and couldn't wait to sink into her sweet pussy. And he'd even take the time to make sure it was slick first.

Fuck.

The first time might be a little too quick for his liking. And maybe even hers. But he'd make sure he made it up to her during the second round.

When they reached the bottom of the stairs, she yanked her arm and screamed, "Stop!"

Zak hesitated and glanced over his shoulder. Her face was red, but he didn't think it was from excitement. No, her eyes were narrowed now as she glared at him.

"Let me go. Right now. I don't think you know who I am."

"Know who you are, but not sure why you're fightin' this... unless you enjoy it? Damn. That could be fun, too."

"No! I baked the cake."

"Well, thank you, babe. Appreciate that. I'm sure it's good. But there's somethin' sweeter than cake I wanna eat first."

She yanked her arm again, but he wasn't letting her go. No way.

"Let. Me. Go."

"Glad Dawg remembered I don't like easy women. Did he coach you on bein' like this?"

"I don't even know who this Dog is."

"*Right.*" Now she really *was* playing some game. "C'mon. Time's a-wastin'." Zak turned to her, grabbed her by the waist and tossed her over his shoulder. She yelped and then gasped at each rushed step he took up the stairs as the air bounced out of her lungs.

Fuck, if all the girls at Heaven's Angels Gentlemen's Club was of her quality, both face and body, business had to be booming and the money rolling into the club coffers.

Having a strip club as one of the businesses under the club umbrella kept all the brothers waist deep in pussy. Money was one benefit, easy access to women was another. Not that there weren't always sweet butts willing to spread their legs for one of the guys at any time. There was. But it was nice to have some variety.

Especially when they were looking like this. Not like they were ridden hard and put away wet.

Zak glanced at the woman he'd thrown over his shoulder. He wondered how many of the other brothers had tasted her charms.

He scowled. He didn't want to think about it.

Tonight, she would just be his. At least until he tired of her and was ready for something fresh.

At the top of the steps, he turned left, assuming it was his old room that the sweet butts had gotten ready. He headed down to the end of the hall as she pounded on his back and yelled curses at him until he opened the last door on the left. Then she got very quiet. With one hand still holding her thighs securely, he banged on the wall until he found the light switch and flipped it on.

He glanced around as the room lit up. Yeah. Stark. Empty. Just the basics. Dresser, bed, lamp, shit like that. Didn't look like anyone had a current claim on his old room. This had to be the one.

He stepped over the threshold and kicked the door closed behind him. Then turned and slid the bolt lock home, making sure they wouldn't be interrupted.

With a grunt, he tossed her onto the bed and her eyes were wild when she landed. Before he could take a step toward the bed, she shouted, "What the fuck!"

"Yeah, that's exactly what we're gonna do," he said, dropping his hand to the button of his jeans.

Sophie looked at the crazy man who was currently stripping off his jeans.

She was going to get fucking raped. *Holy shit*. She needed to get the hell out of there.

She never should've agreed to make these bikers a cake for someone coming home from prison. That should've been a red flag right there.

But she'd been desperate for business.

Damn, and now she was in trouble. All because she couldn't pass up the hundred bucks they offered for a sheet cake for some convict named Zak.

Unfortunately, there was only one way out of this room and this insane man was standing between her and it. She quickly swept the room with her gaze. She couldn't find even a damn window to jump from.

She scrambled backwards toward the top of the bed, trying to at least put some distance between them.

But he didn't look worried that she might not be a willing participant, the guy kept getting more and more naked.

Hell… how his face looked, how his body looked—and she was seeing *way* too much of it already—he had no reason to need to take a woman against her will. But even though he looked good on the outside, he might be a bastard on the inside. A mean one at that.

"Hate to say this but..." He inhaled a breath. "Been ten years, babe, so first time's gonna be quick. An' when I say quick, I mean instant. The second time... hopefully, not so much."

Second time?

Christ, he already had plans to assault her at least twice.

"So, apologizin' now, but I'll make it up to you, make it worth that minute-man routine beforehand. Then afterward... Afterward, if you don't think my foreplay was worth it an' I disappointed you, then you can bitch me out. I'll understand. But lemme make this clear, *I need this*. Desperately. So, sorry I'm gonna be quick, but also appreciate you bein' my first of the night."

First of the night?

Who says those types of things? Serial rapists?

Then some of his other words began to permeate her brain. Foreplay, bitch him out. Ten years.

This just had to be a huge misunderstanding. He thought she was someone else. She simply needed to clear that up.

"I think you're mistaken—"

"No, pretty damn sure I'm gonna be quick. So, might wanna start takin' off your clothes."

Yeah, she'd get right on that. "That's not going to happen. At least not without a fight."

He paused at the end of the bed, his thumbs tucked in the elastic waist of his boxers. He tilted his head and studied her. "You like it rough?"

What? No!

Well, sometimes... *What the fuck!* What was she thinking?

"I'm the baker."

He cocked an eyebrow. "Baker? Weird name for a stripper." He shrugged. "But whatever." And with that, he dropped his boxers to his ankles and stepped out of them.

Sophie swallowed hard. That wasn't the only thing hard. She

couldn't pull her gaze away from his erection. Long, thick, a gleam from his precum at the tip.

It *had* been awhile since—

She slapped herself mentally. Yes, it had been a while for her, but she wasn't that desperate to take this tattooed biker who thought she was a stripper, apparently, to bed.

She'd lost her ever-loving mind.

But the man was already naked. And, no matter what, he looked damn good. Even covered in all those tattoos. Probably prison tattoos. *Ugh.*

But... What would it hurt to bang out a good orgasm with the guy? It's not like she'd ever see him again. She could mail the bill for the cake.

That's when she remembered the cake was still out in the car. Crap.

"Just gonna sit there starin', or you gonna get naked?"

It was like the devil sat on one of her shoulders, an angel on the other. Completely at war with each other.

He put a knee on the bed and his cock bobbed. She found herself mesmerized.

She made a mental note to buy more batteries for her vibrator, because it could only be desperation making her think it was a good idea to fuck this guy. Especially after she thought he was going to assault her.

Which he didn't. Yet.

He hadn't even touched her since dropping her on the bed.

Her eyes flicked to the locked door. She could probably leave if she wanted to.

Her eyes flicked back to his honed chest full of badass tats.

Did she want to?

He waved a hand in front of her face. "Anybody in there? Like it rough, I can give it to you rough, babe. Like it sweet, I can give it to you sweet. Just say the word, but like I said, you probably won't have much of a choice the first time. The second, though... Just sayin'. However, first, wanna eat your pussy like it's the buffet at Hoss's. You into that?"

Sophie suddenly pictured his face with its closely trimmed beard between her thighs in her mind's eye. And for some reason, her body began to overheat and get slick.

Holy fuck, she was going to let this man put his lips to hers. And not the ones on her face, either.

She had gone off the deep end. Truly, just lost all her marbles.

No one saw them come up here. She could have a couple orgasms, finish delivering the cake and then hightail it out of here, never to see this guy again. It would stay between him and her.

Right?

Yeah.

Her pulse thumped in her neck as she pulled her sweater over her head, moved to her knees and wiggled down her jeans and panties at the same time until they got to her ankles. She kicked off her shoes and socks, peeled her pants over her feet, then reached behind her to release her bra.

Fuck it. No one knew her here. It might not have been ten years for her, but it had been long enough that she was no longer picky. At least for tonight. Because normally she wouldn't have been caught dead with a man like him, in a place like this.

"You Zak?" she finally asked him, thinking of the name she had piped on the cake in red icing. It also said, "Welcome home."

"Yep."

So not only was she now willingly going to fuck a biker, she was fucking a known convict.

Holy Hannah, her life choices had gone down the shitter.

"Are you good at eating pussy?" she asked, sliding down the bed now that she was totally naked.

"Used to be," came his answer as he stared at her breasts while he had a hand gripped tightly around his cock.

"Think you can remember how to do it well?" she asked, bending her knees and parting her thighs.

"I'll do my damnedest, babe."

"Stop talking and do it then," she said, lying back against the pillow, but holding her head up enough that she could watch him.

His eyes widened as they moved from her chest to her face. He hesitated at her demand, then a wide smile crawled across his face. In seconds, he had his face buried between her legs and the brush of his beard against her skin made her gasp.

When his lips sucked at her clit, her hips shot off the bed. One heavy arm came across them to hold her down while the man went to town on her. Licking, flicking, sucking, nipping, working her into a mindless frenzy.

Fuck yes, he knew how to eat pussy. *Damn.*

Long, callused fingers slid between her folds, while his mouth never left her sensitive nub. He stroked and stroked… and stroked as she opened for him and then slid two fingers inside her.

"So fuckin' wet, babe," he murmured against her and the vibrations of his words made her cry out and thrash against him.

When he curled his fingers and found her spot, her head fell back, her body arched and pulsated around his digits, squeezing, trying to draw him deeper.

"That's one," he said.

She had to admit that it was a good one.

When his prickly beard scraped her pussy and clit, she had number two. She was trying to catch her breath when he moved over her, his cock prodding between her slick, swollen lips and she spread her legs even wider, inviting him to take her.

"Condom," she panted. But, holy hell, she wanted him inside her… like yesterday!

"Damn," he grumbled as he scrambled to find one in the drawer of the nightstand by the bed. "Oh, thank fuck," he said, holding up a condom.

"Hurry up," she demanded.

"Don't have to tell me twice, babe. Told you it won't take me long."

"That's not what I meant."

"I know. But that's how it's gonna be. 'Specially after tastin' your sweet honey."

The crown of his latex-encased cock bumped against her, then he slid inside slowly. And, damn, did he fill her up.

They both sighed at the same time as he fully seated himself, then stilled.

He sandwiched her face between his palms and met her eyes. His were dark, so dark, but didn't falter as he stared at her. "Thank you, babe, for bein' so damn tight."

Was that a compliment?

Then his eyes hooded and he began to move. She quickly forgot the weird compliment, wrapping her legs around his hips, matching his rhythm, determined to climax one more time before he did. She had a feeling she'd have to move fast, so she shoved a hand between them and thumbed her clit as his pace picked up and he began to pound her, throwing his head back and grimacing.

"Jesus," slipped from his lips. "Not goin' to... Ah, fuck. Fuck. Fuck. I told you... Christ. You feel so good, babe. Can't even..."

His body tensed and he dropped his forehead to hers, his breathing fast and ragged between his parted lips.

Sophie pressed harder on her clit, frantically trying to beat him to the end. He wasn't going to last much longer. He was right. He was going to be lightning quick.

But then he slammed his hips against her, which made an orgasm ripple from the tip of her toes all the way to her core and she exploded at the same time he did.

"Fuck," he cried out. She echoed the same curse, though silently since she'd lost all the oxygen from her lungs. He drove deep a couple more times, then collapsed on top of her, barely holding his weight up on his forearms.

His cheek landed on her breast like it was a pillow and his words vibrated against her, "Nice to see real tits on a stripper. Must be comin' back in style. Always hated the fake ones."

Sophie closed her eyes, struggling to take a calming breath before she beat the fuck out of him.

When his thumb brushed back and forth across her nipple, she tensed, jammed her fingers into his hair and yanked his head up about to give him the *what for.* As she opened her mouth and took a deep breath, a pounding at the door stopped her in her tracks.

ZAK JERKED at the sound of pounding on the door. Who the fuck would be interrupting them at this moment? He was sure the noises coming from the room would have been loud enough to make it clear to anyone that they'd been busy and wouldn't want to be disturbed.

"Brother, got your girls," a gruff, loud voice, followed by a chuckle seeped through the door.

Dawg.

Zak's eyes slid from the door back to the woman underneath him. Her eyes were wide, and she looked a bit angry. Yeah, more than a bit.

Hell, it wasn't like he enjoyed being interrupted either.

He reluctantly slipped from her warm, wet, tight body.

"Don't move an inch," he warned her in a low growl as he rolled off her, yanked on his boxers and moved to the door, glancing back to make sure she had the sheet pulled over her.

He slid the bolt lock open and cracked the door. Dawg had three women hanging off him and wore an enormous grin.

Three.

Dawg's eyes shot to the bed as the man pushed the door open wider and his grin turned into a knowing smile. "Fuck. Looks like you found your own."

The women with Dawg were obviously strippers. The hair, the make-up, slutty clothing. Ridiculously high, ankle-breaking platform heels.

And those fucking fake breasts. Something Zak despised.

He didn't have to look back at the bed to know he might have... could have... *possibly* made a mistake.

A big one. One he had a feeling he was going to pay for.

"Yeah, brother, I'm good for now," he finally said.

One of the strippers, the blonde, pouted and the other two, a redhead and a brunette, frowned and made noises of complaint.

With a snort, Dawg shrugged. "No sweat off my balls, more for the rest of us. Let's go, ladies." He steered his mini-harem around, leading them down the hallway. "Give her a good one for me, too. She looks sweet," Dawg shot over his shoulder.

Zak didn't answer, instead slowly shut the door, carefully slid the bolt home again, then stared at the door for a heartbeat, then two. Then another one for good measure.

Sucking in a breath, he turned. She now sat up in bed, the sheet clutched to her chest. And if looks could kill, he'd be not only six feet under, but so far under he'd be incinerated at the Earth's core.

"You're not one of Dawg's girls," he mentioned, feeling like Captain Obvious.

"No."

"Who are you?"

"I tried to tell you."

Zak took two steps toward the bed, repeating, "Who are you?" The tone in his voice left no doubt he wanted an answer, and he wanted it now.

Her eyes narrowed at his tone. "I baked your cake."

No shit. He shook his head and dragged fingers through his hair. "You already said that."

"I own a bakery. I was asked to deliver a cake. Sorry I was late but I had car trouble." She pushed herself out of bed and snagged her bra that had landed on the bedside lamp when she tossed it earlier, yanking it on and fastening it with jerky movements. "I figured I'd get a tip, but I wasn't expecting one like this." Her words came slightly muffled as she tugged her sweater over her head.

"Got more than the tip." Then Zak grimaced at his own unfiltered response. *Fuck.* He wouldn't blame her if she shanked him for that.

Her pointed gaze bounced off him to search the room and when she spotted her panties, she moved to yank them on. "Yes, and now I'm going to get dressed and leave. I'll send a bill for the balance owed. Just so you know, I'll be tacking on a nice generous tip."

Fuck.

Zak pinched the bridge of his nose as a thought began to claw at him. "It's important you don't tell anyone 'bout this."

The last thing he needed was to be falsely accused of rape. Though, he now admitted he hadn't paid attention to the signs she had displayed of her reluctance to his *charms*. But he had been so worked up for his first taste of pussy in ten years, he hadn't been thinking straight.

And sweet pussy it was. Not only that, she ended up coming three times, so she had to enjoy it, right?

He frowned.

If she got a hair up her ass about what happened enough to bitch about it to anyone listening, he might end up in cuffs and then stuffed back in that fucking concrete box. The one he vowed never to go back to.

He wouldn't survive this time.

His relief at her next words overwhelmed him. "I won't be shouting it from the rooftops, if that's what you're thinking."

Zak paused, his mind suddenly doing a total one-eighty. Was she saying he sucked? Well, he might have been a bit rusty, but... No, she had more than one orgasm in an admittedly very short amount of time. "Why? Wasn't good enough for you?"

After tugging on her jeans and slipping on her shoes, she straightened, but didn't answer.

And suddenly he worried about his technique. Maybe he *had* been rusty. *Damn.*

"Answer me. A biker like me ain't good 'nough for you? Or was it just me in general?"

She dropped her hands to her hips and squared off. "I prefer my men a little more..." Her voice drifted away. On purpose. She was trying to plant doubts in his mind about his performance.

"What?" he prodded.

She raised a hand and drew a line in the air from the top of his head all the way down to his toes. "Not this."

Not this.

"More sophisticated?"

"Right."

"No tattoos?"

"Uh huh."

"Not a felon," he continued.

Her eyes widened, but she schooled her face quickly. "Definitely not."

"Bet your preferred type of man don't get you off as many times as I did."

She lifted a shoulder, then went to push past him. "Sometimes you have to take the bad with the good."

He snagged her arm and pulled her close, dropping his face close to hers. "Sometimes you gotta take the good with the *bad*."

He didn't miss her flinch. Then, her face turned to stone again, only her green eyes flashing. "Well, I have to go. Thank you for the orgasms—"

"Zak."

"That's right, the name on the cake. Welcome home from prison, Zak. The bill will be in the mail." She yanked on her arm, but he refused to release her.

"I'll walk you out," he gritted from between clenched teeth.

"I'll be fine," she said tightly.

"Sure, if you don't mind endin' up in another one of these rooms with another *dirty* biker." He smiled. "Or maybe you do want that, babe. Or... maybe you wanna hit me up for the second round I promised you."

She stiffened. "You may escort me out."

"Thought so." Though, he was a bit disappointed she wasn't eager to jump back in bed and let him hit that sweet, succulent pussy again.

And after being with her, he had no desire to hit up one of the girls that had been hanging off Dawg.

AFTER SHOVING the sheet cake at him, she had climbed into her car and sat there, watching the man swagger back to the building.

Swagger.

The man actually swaggered. He had a roll to his hips that made him even better in bed than a man had a right to be. Even if he had been out of practice from being locked up for the past ten years.

Fuck me.

Her hand went to her breast where it still stung from his bite. His mark. She smiled.

Fuck him.

She made some big mistakes in her life, but tonight...

Fuck.

Tonight might have been her biggest.

And best.

But as long as nobody found out about it she was golden. He got what he wanted. She got a couple—okay, *three*—orgasms that weren't self-induced. And she made money on a cake. And you bet she was adding one healthy tip onto the balance.

For almost a whole second she regretted not going for the second round.

Chapter Three

ACE HELD out the keys to the clubhouse. "Keys to the kingdom."

Zak ignored them, shaking his head. "Don't deserve them."

Ace tossed them his way and Zak had no choice but to catch the heavy responsibility that was disguised as a set of keys.

"The hell you don't. Soon as the officers meet, you'll be wearin' the prez patch again."

Zak dropped his gaze to the toes of his heavy black boots and shook his head once more. Though after tying on a big one last night after the baker lady left, it hurt every time he did so. "Can't upset the order."

Baker lady. He didn't even know her fucking name. And she only knew his because she had decorated his cake for the pig roast. Damn.

"It's already expected. Won't be a surprise to anyone."

Zak leveled his gaze at Ace, who had stepped in as a father figure for him when his own blood had disowned him for following in his grandfather's footsteps. "Again, I don't deserve it. Been away too long."

"Don't sell yourself short. This club's in your blood. Your grandfather was a founding member. Hell, he was ground zero."

"Pierce—" Zak started.

"Pierce's doing an okay job, but he ain't you. You had a vision for this club even though you were young. Progressive. Knew what was needed, what *needs* done."

Zak looked around, glad that church was empty and quiet this morning. The rooms upstairs were full, naked bodies sprawled over beds. Some of the brothers with more than one woman draped over them like blankets.

They'd have worse hangovers than Zak. Guaranteed. Ace wasn't a big drinker, so he had clear eyes and a clear head this morning versus Zak's slightly fuzzy one.

Zak cocked an eyebrow and headed over to the commercial-sized coffeemaker in the corner of the room. "Why didn't they vote you in as president?"

The large man, who now had to be in his early to mid-fifties, pushed past him to yank coffee filters and a huge bag of ground coffee from the overhead cabinet. He turned and shrugged. "Didn't want it. Need young blood to run this club right. To take it out of the old ways, the outlaw ways. Make it respectable, like you—and some of the rest of us—wanted. Anyhow, between takin' care of the farm, my mother, my kids, the brothers, running the pawn shop, and, not to mention, handlin' the funds of this club, I have enough responsibility hangin' 'round my fuckin' neck. Plus, Janice would've probably divorced my ass if I had."

The scent of the coffee grounds seeped into Zak's nostrils making him inhale deeply. Quality coffee. It had been a long time since he drank a decent cup that wasn't watered down.

"How is she?"

Ace finished setting up the coffeemaker, flipped the switch, then turned to shove an empty mug at Zak. "Good. Can't wait to see you. Wants you to come to dinner. Hell, wants you to move into one of the empty cabins at the farm instead of stayin' in one of the rooms upstairs."

Zak studied the worn, scratched Harley emblem on the mug, not meeting Ace's eyes. "That what you want?"

"It's whatever you want, Zak. You're like a son to me. Only want what's best for you."

He finally met the older man's gaze. "An' the club."

"An' the club," Ace repeated. "My father started this damn thing with your grandfather. Now Bear's been gone a long time an' Doc will never see the light of day again."

A tragic end to both fellow soldiers and best friends.

"How's he doin' down at Greene?" Unlike Fayette where Zak had been housed, Greene was a max security prison. Prisoners deemed violent and convicted capital cases ended up there.

"He's a seventy-four-year-old Vietnam vet who was," Ace shook his head, "*is* an' always will be an outlaw biker in his own mind. So how do you think he's doin'? He's a cantankerous old man who thinks he can rule the roost in a prison full of thugs an' skinheads."

"An' is he?"

Ace boomed out a laugh, the corners of his eyes crinkling. "Yeah, that old fucker sure is."

That drew a smile from Zak. "I'll have to make sure to go visit him soon."

"No. Stay away from that prison. He'll understand if you don't come by. He knows what happened."

Zak scowled but nodded. "Still..."

When Bear, Zak's grandfather, was killed by another outlaw biker back in the early eighties, his fellow Army buddy and co-founder of DAMC, set out for revenge. And Doc didn't do it discreetly or quietly. He took out a few members of their rival club, the Shadow Warriors, in the process. As did Zak's uncle, Rocky.

That caused a permanent, volatile wedge between the two clubs and landed Doc in prison for life without parole and left Lonnie, his wife, raising Ace, Allie and Annie by herself. Though the club helped out. Especially financially. That's why it was so important to keep the coffers fat and overflowing. For shit like that.

"Your mom good?"

Ace sighed. "Yeah, she's just as cantankerous as Pop, but, unfortunately, I have to deal with it since she's livin' in the farmhouse with me an' Janice. Allie and Annie both live in cabins on the property. We all help take care of Mom."

Ace's sisters had to be in their late forties by now. Hell, maybe even getting close to fifty.

"That was a hell of a homecomin' last night, wasn't it." Not a question, more of a fact.

"Sure was," Zak murmured, watching the dark brew drip into the glass coffee pot.

"You disappeared for a while. Get some tail?"

Zak turned away to hide his face. "Yeah."

Ace clapped him on the back then strode past him to the back door. "Gotta go open up the shop. Need anything, let me know. Be back later for the officer's meetin'."

Zak groaned as Ace shut the door behind him, cutting off the bright morning light which made him squint from his hangover.

He grabbed the steaming pot of coffee and filled his mug, then carefully took a sip. He never liked black coffee before going into the joint. In there, he learned to appreciate it. Though, he hadn't had much of a choice.

He sighed after swallowing the hot, rich brew and settled on one of the old, worn couches that sat around the edge of the room. Some days and nights this room would be packed. Members, their ol' ladies, prospects and hang-arounds filling every corner, every seat. Playing pool, darts, cards, drinking at the private club bar, or just plain raising hell.

But right now, everyone was nursing their throbbing heads or still passed out.

Zak studied the DAMC's emblem over the bar. His granddaddy had carved it out of a single, solid piece of wood. He'd heard Bear had been good with a knife. And the craftsmanship in the curves and lines of the sign showed just how much.

All Zak wanted to do was follow in his grandfather's footsteps. The man had been a legend in his time.

Just because his father and brother followed a different path, a straighter path, didn't mean he had to. His Uncle Rocky didn't either. And Zak had looked up to his uncle, even though it infuriated his father that he had done so. Mitch told young Zak time and time again that he shouldn't revere his outlaw uncle.

But this club was in his blood. He was born a part of it. Whether his parents liked it or not.

Mitch and Ace almost got into a knock-down brawl one day when Zak was about twelve. Zak had snuck out of the house to go for a ride on the back of Ace's Harley. By the end of that long ride over winding roads, through valleys, over mountains, Zak knew where his future laid.

He asked for a motorcycle every Christmas, every birthday. Finally, his dad got him a mini-bike and later a dirt bike. Same for Axel. His father might not have liked some aspects of the DAMC, but he loved to ride, too, so in the end he didn't deny his boys the pleasure. Axel finally followed in his footsteps, heading off to the police academy and finally joining the Shadow Valley PD like their father. Both were members of the Blue Avengers MC, a club for cops.

They could deny it all they want but the club was in their blood, too. However, due to their chosen profession, trying to stay on the straight and narrow, they couldn't ride with the Dirty Angels. No. Instead, they started their own club, one that law enforcement supported and participated in.

It wasn't like Zak didn't understand why they kept themselves separated. Back in the day, the MC was into some serious shit.

Death, destruction and mayhem were a normal part of the game. Prison time was as common as a blink of the eye. When you were in a club, it was expected, respected.

Now, through the years, the club tried to clean up its act. Move onto legit businesses, take part in charities, help the community. Try to get a better image.

And it wasn't because there wasn't a choice. There was a choice. But getting rid of the one percenter image helped keep the coffers full. Less members were spending time in the joint which meant more hands on deck.

Another benefit was it helped keep law enforcement off their ass and out of their business.

And that's why he was voted in as president when he was twenty, which was unheard of. Zak had a vision for this club to take them into the future. Be progressive, like Ace said. And like Ace, he only wanted the best for this club and his brothers.

He stared at the bottom of his now empty mug. He needed another cup of coffee and wondered if there was any of that cake left from last night to go along with it. He only got a chance to drag a finger through the icing and the sweetness on his tongue reminded him of her.

The one whose name he didn't know.

The one who baked him a damn cake. *And* spelled his name correctly on it.

And had that goddamn hair he wanted to wrap his fists in and pull as he was fucking her from behind.

He couldn't stop fantasizing about her pink, full lips circling the base of his cock, leaving a lipstick ring. If she even wore lipstick.

Fuck.

His cock stirred and he rubbed at the crotch of his jeans. That quickie wasn't enough last night. It had only been a taste of what he wanted to do with a woman.

No, not with a woman.

With her.

Goddamn it. One taste of her pussy and he was hooked.

He could wait until the bill showed up in the mail to find out who she was or he could find out on his own.

He still wanted his second round with her. And he hoped she wanted the same.

Because if not... Zak blew out a breath. He'd just have to convince her otherwise.

WHEN THE DOOR to the meeting room finally flung open, the members who made up the Executive Committee filed out. Not one of them looked happy.

Not one.

Not Ace, not Jag, not the Sergeant at Arms Diesel, not Zak's former but still current VP Hawk. Even Dex, the club Secretary, walked out shaking his head. The only person who hadn't crossed the threshold yet was Pierce, the still—from how everyone's face looked—current sitting president.

In one way he was relieved, he hadn't been tapped to replace Pierce. Being in a motorcycle club could be its own form of prison. It was hard to be alone or completely free of club business. And it was worse when you were at the top.

But in another way, Zak was disappointed. He knew Pierce preferred the old ways. That's why when word got back to him that he'd been voted in after Zak got locked up he'd been surprised.

Most likely, no one else wanted the job. And he couldn't blame any of them.

Now that Pierce had been heading the club for the last ten years, Zak doubted he wanted to step down.

He didn't have any personal beef with Pierce. He was a brother like any other. And at forty-nine, the man had been a member a lot longer than Zak or most of the other guys. So, he'd seen the club go through a lot of shit and a lot of changes.

Zak heard his name yelled from within the meeting room. He met Ace's eyes before stepping through the door.

"Shut it."

He did, then turned to face the reigning president sitting at the head of the long, lacquered wood table his grandfather also hand carved with the club's emblem.

"I didn't ask for this vote," Zak started.

Pierce stared at him for a few moments, his dark eyes unreadable. "I know. But just 'cause you're out don't mean I'll step down an' hand the reins back over."

Zak didn't answer. He waited. The man wasn't done saying his piece.

"Got no ill will toward you, Z. But you know I was one who thought you were too young to become president all those years ago.

Just 'cause your granddaddy was one of the founders don't mean you should automatically be prez. But you do got a lick of sense." He hesitated, then shook his head. "Or at least, thought so until you went up river to Fayette. Now that was a fuckin' stupid move."

"Wasn't my choice."

"No shit." Pierce shook his head again, laying his hands flat on the table in front of him and studying them for a second before looking back up at Zak. "I've always understood where you were comin' from, where Ace was comin' from when you talked about takin' this club into the future, just know that. Not sayin' I agree with everything. But the club's doing well, so I hafta admit it works. Our membership's up. Money's rollin' in. Hell, might hafta start our own armored car biz." He snorted. "If Hawk wasn't a damn good VP, I'd make you mine. But he is, so you ain't. Got me?"

"Yeah, got you."

"Don't mean I don't appreciate your ideas. Hell, we need fresh ideas. We just had a lil convo about opening the club up to a few more prospects. The upside is cheap labor for the businesses. The downside?" Pierce shrugged. "The downside is that they're prospects an' just a step above the bitches that hang around here."

Zak kept his mouth shut.

"Anyway, here are my words to you as prez. Heed them well... As you know, there's a hierarchy here, an' it's important it's followed. Anarchy does us no good, no matter what the reason. This is the one an' only time you get a chance to walk away scot free. No buy-out. Don't like how things are bein' run? Go patch a different club. Join a monastery. Take a trip to fuckin' Disney World. Don't give a shit what you do. But if you stay an' don't follow the rules, there will be consequences. An' I'm sure as shit I don't need to tell you what they are.

"Right now, you're wearin' our cut. That could change. Our colors on your back could be removed easily with a knife or a torch. An' I'm not talkin' 'bout the one on your cut. Remember that. Then remember the one who holds the gavel. That's all I ask."

"Yeah," Zak said, not breaking their locked gaze. "Got it. Got one question though."

"Shoot."

"You gonna keep takin' this club forward? Or you wanna take it back?"

"This ain't your granddaddy's club no more, Z. I doubt we could go back that far. Hafta admit, what you fought for works. But do I like we've been pussified? No. It ain't good for our rep. We still have too many rivals out there. Not only the Warriors but the Dark Knights. We'll do whatever we fuckin' need to do to keep our territory. If it can't be handled on the up and up, then we'll do it on the down low. Got me?"

"Yeah."

Pierce pushed up and away from the table. "So, you stayin'?"

"Yeah." There was no way he was walking away. Pierce as prez or not.

"Then I'll give you a week to get your shit in order. You got your room upstairs, but you need to pick a place to work, pay your dues, make sure your sled's ready to ride as soon as the weather breaks. An' don't try to upset the order. Got me?"

"Yeah."

Pierce smiled and made his way around the table. They clasped forearms, bumped shoulders and Pierce slapped him on the back. "You wanna work at the gun shop, just say so. I could use the help."

"Felon, Pierce," Zak reminded him.

"Aw, shit. Right. Fuck. Ain't right, but you gotta live with it now."

He sure did. It was something that would mark him for life.

"Hey, one more question," Zak asked as Pierce draped an arm over his shoulders and they headed toward the door.

"What's that?"

"That cake last night. Where'd you all get it?"

"The fuck if I know, check with Grizz's ol' lady. Thinkin' she ordered it. Fuckin' shit was good though, wasn't it?"

Zak nodded, fighting a smile as they walked out into the clubhouse and joined his brothers at the bar.

Chapter Four

SOPHIE DOUBLE CHECKED the counters to make sure anything edible had been put away and that any stray crumbs had been wiped clean so they wouldn't attract ants, or mice. She shuddered at the thought of a rodent running through her bakery. She wiped her hands on her apron, then pulled it over her head and threw it in the laundry bag to be washed.

With a sigh of relief that the long day was finally over, she moved toward the front of the shop to lock the door before heading up to shower and collapse on her bed. She needed sleep because she had to do this all over again tomorrow.

As an adult, her dream had always been to open her own business. In her teens, her passion had been baking in her grandmother's kitchen. Learning the ins and outs of baking sweet treats from her grandmother that made people smile. Whether cakes, cookies, brownies, cupcakes, whatever.

So, when her grandmother died last year and left her the bulk of her estate, she decided to do something with that money to make her dream come true. It wasn't a fortune, no. But it was enough of a nest egg to buy a building in a town where the real estate and taxes were reasonable, but also where the population was large enough to sustain the business.

And that's how she landed in Shadow Valley, a half hour south west of Pittsburgh. She hadn't been looking in the area since she was from Philadelphia, but when her real estate agent called to say she found the perfect business—a turnkey bakery that included all the equipment and even had an apartment above it for her to live in—she couldn't resist.

Not in her right mind.

The only problem was she had no family or friends nearby.

As she reached to twist the deadbolt, the door flew open making the bells above it clank in protest. With a yelp, she fell back, losing her balance and landing with a thud on her ass. Her heart froze in her chest before thumping wildly all the way into her throat.

What the hell?

Trying to catch her breath, she looked up to see a man standing over her, legs spread wide, hand reaching out.

"Sorry," he grumbled. "Was tryin' to catch you before you locked me out. Didn't mean to knock you down like that."

Sophie's gaze bounced from the outstretched hand to that damn biker's eyes. *Holy hell.*

She swallowed, gathered her wits, and pushed herself to her feet, ignoring his offer of help.

"You okay?" His deep, gravelly voice almost pulled a shudder from her. Almost.

Sophie brushed off her ass and frowned. "You couldn't have just knocked?"

"I knock, doubt you'd let me in."

He had that right. But she scowled anyway.

He dropped his hand then turned on his biker booted heel to lock the deadbolt.

Oh. No.

Last time he locked a door they ended up naked, and she'd had three unplanned orgasms.

She tilted her head and studied him as he swung back to face her. Though, those orgasms hadn't been such a bad thing. He was just the wrong person to have them with.

He smiled as if he'd read her mind.

She ran a hand over her throat, and breathed deeply, trying to keep her pulse from leaping out of her neck.

"What are you doing here?"

"Your name is Sophie."

Sophie opened her mouth then snapped it shut. He wasn't asking. He was telling her what her own name was.

Genius.

"Yes, it's on the two-foot-high sign out front. A little obvious."

He lifted one shoulder. "This place used to be Martin's Bakery."

She shook her head slightly, confused. "Yeah, so?"

"My mom used to bring me here when I was a tyke. Loved their whoopie pies."

"Chocolate ones with the vanilla icing?"

A corner of his mouth slid up into a half smile. "Yeah. Had to be. Only the original."

Damn, the man was not only hot, he was endearing when remembering his youth. He was probably a lot more innocent back then than he was now. She pictured him wearing cute tan shorts, a little blue polo shirt, and holding onto his mother's hand as she brought him in for his favorite treat.

Now...

Oh yeah. That innocent little boy grew up and now wore black jeans, heavy black leather boots, a worn black leather vest that had some filthy patches sewn on, over a white long-sleeved thermal shirt. And a big, thick black leather belt held closed by a silver buckle with an emblem etched into it circled his waist.

She wondered if he'd mind if she bent over to peek at it a little closer. She was curious what the emblem was.

She winced at her thoughts.

"You make 'em?"

What?

Oh. Yeah... "No."

"Can you?"

"Probably. You placing an order?"

"Maybe."

Sophie pursed her lips and ran her gaze over his short beard and shaggy dark brown hair. She squeezed her thighs together in an attempt to get rid of the memory of that beard scraping along her inner thighs and against her pussy.

Fuck, woman, get your shit together, this man's a *felon*. A felon! He probably killed someone.

Frowning, Sophie swallowed hard as his deep blue eyes pinned her. The man had some thick eyelashes. He sure did. *Damn.*

What a shame he was a felon *and* a biker. Not to mention, she was new in town and trying to run a respectable business. Last thing she wanted was to chase away clientele by having bikers parking out front and coming into her shop. Or climbing into her bed.

He *could* park out back.

What? No!

No. No. No.

And when he smiled again she just about melted onto the floor. She needed to get her shit together. Immediately.

"Zak, right?"

"Yes, ma'am."

She cocked an eyebrow at his ma'am before continuing. "You here for a reason?"

"Sure am."

She waited.

Nothing.

"Aaaaaaaand that reason is..."

"To settle our bill."

She arched an eyebrow in his direction. "You're paying for your own cake?"

He didn't answer, just stepped toward her. She stepped back.

"Club's payin' for it."

"Ah. Okay. I did say I'd drop it in the mail."

"Yeah."

"But if you want to settle it now, we can do that."

He lifted his chin. It was a sort of nod. Not quite. But Sophie had to assume he was agreeing with her. He certainly was a man of few words.

Her brows knitted, she took a breath, then turned to head to the back of the shop where the opening was in the counter to go behind the glass display case. She lifted the section of the counter that had hinges, stepped through and when she turned to drop it behind her, he was right there.

Right. There.

Damn. How was the man so quiet in those heavy boots?

"Jesus," she whispered.

"Nah. Zak."

She blinked, then pressed her lips flat, trying not to laugh. His eyes crinkled at the corners and he pushed past her to go behind the counter and display case. Where only employees were allowed, that was if she had some.

"Uh..." She guessed it didn't matter since the shop was closed.

"How long you been here?" he asked, not bothering to look at her.

"Six months."

"You're not from here, otherwise I'd know you. Where you from?" He explored the area behind the display case, running a finger over the counter, touching stuff, peeking in bowls. Simply being nosey.

She didn't have to answer his questions. No, she did not.

"Not here," she finally answered.

He stilled, then glanced over his shoulder at her. "What kind of answer's that?"

"One you're getting."

"One I won't accept."

"It's as good as you're going to get."

He turned, crossing his thick, thermal covered arms over his chest. That's when she noticed the spot where a patch was missing. The leather was cleaner, darker, in that rectangular area and a few white threads had been left behind.

"What happened?" she asked, jerking her chin in the area of his missing patch.

"Prison."

Sophie's nostrils flared as she sucked in a breath. Yes, that's right. They were celebrating his "homecoming" last night. "So, what'd you do?"

"Nothin'."

Right. "I'm sure the prison is full of people who were just doing *nothin'*."

He didn't answer but leaned back against the display case, his arms still crossed. "Worried?"

"About what?"

"Me. Hurtin' you."

She hesitated and studied his eyes, which watched her carefully. They appeared clear, alert. The hairs on the back of her neck didn't rise. Her gut instinct was no, he wouldn't hurt her. "Should I be?"

"Nope."

Sophie nodded. "Okay."

"Just that simple."

"What?"

"I say I'm not gonna hurt you an' you say okay. You accept that as truth."

"Why not?"

"'Cause you don't know me."

"Hold on—"

"No, babe, accepted my answer too easily. Hardly fought me last night..."

"No," she corrected, shaking her head vehemently. "I fought you."

"Hardly," he repeated with a frown. "An' now you just accept my word that I won't hurt you. Woman, need to be more careful."

"Of men like you?"

His voice lowered an octave. "Yeah, men like me."

When he pushed off the display and straightened, Sophie stepped back, keeping their distance. "Make up your mind. Last night you weren't happy when I said I wasn't thrilled about doing a biker. Tonight, you're not happy I would." Sophie winced at her own words. *Damn it.*

He cocked a brow and smiled. "You wanna do me?"

"I didn't mean it like that."

"How'd you mean it?"

"Let me just find the bill. Once you settle it, you can leave. Please." She was going to have to get by him to go up to the front. The pending invoices were in a folder on a shelf under the cash register.

He didn't move out of the way when she cautiously approached. In fact, he seemed to spread out, block her path. He wanted her to squeeze by him.

"Excuse me," she said, avoiding his eyes.

"Sophie," he said softly.

She wouldn't look up into those blue eyes of his. She would not. Nope. She focused on her destination, the register. "You're in my way," she whispered.

"Yeah," he answered on a breath.

A thumb came under her chin and tilted her face up until she couldn't avoid those beautiful eyes of his.

"Don't like your hair like that," he murmured.

Her hand automatically went to her head. "My ponytail?" she asked, surprised. When she worked she always had it pulled up in some fashion.

"Though, could be great for when you're givin' me head. Somethin' for me to hold on to."

Sophie's mouth dropped open.

"But like it better when it's fallin' down 'round your tits an' your nipples are peekin' out."

What. The...

Heat exploded in her belly and landed in her groin. That was nowhere near a romantic statement but, damn, did it turn her on.

Right now, it wasn't such a good idea to be standing so close to him. She shoved past him, yanking her chin from his grasp. She quickly grabbed the folder and slammed it on top of the display case, thumbing through it until she found the bill for his *got-sprung-from-the-slammer* cake. Grabbing a red pen, she scribbled a tip onto the balance and held out the bill to him.

With a half grin, he plucked it from her fingers and glanced at it. Then glanced at it again, the cocky grin gone.

She waited for him to complain, to bitch about the exorbitant amount she just tacked on. But he didn't say a word.

No, instead he dug out a long leather wallet from his back pocket. A freaking wallet that actually had a chain attached to one of his belt loops. Jeez, was he living in the seventies?

He opened the wallet and snagged two bills out of it, handing them to her. She stared at the two hundred dollars he offered.

Two hundred bucks. That wasn't even the amount she had written in red ink. That was twice as much.

Without a word, she plucked the money from his fingers, opened the register and tucked the money inside.

"Should put that in a safe, not leave it out here."

As she jammed the cash drawer closed, she mumbled, "Thanks for the business advice."

"Nothing to do with business. Has to do with keepin' you safe."

Sophie bit her bottom lip hard, but released it before turning to face him, hands on her hips.

She tilted her head, frowning. "What do you care about my safety?"

"Just a suggestion," he said simply.

"Right."

"My town. Want to keep it safe. You live in my town. You work in my town. Want to keep you safe, too."

"*Your* town?"

"Yeah, Shadow Valley's Dirty Angels territory."

"I thought it was Shadow Valley PD territory."

"Unfortunately, we gotta share."

Huh.

"Okay, well, you're all paid up. Now you can go. Thanks for the generous tip." She shot him a fake smile, then went to move past him, but he snagged her upper arm and pulled her close.

"Sophie," was all he said low and growly causing her pussy to clench. Damn body. Always betraying her. For once, she wished it would betray her with the right man. Not the wrong one who was holding onto her way too tightly. She yanked her arm, but he didn't let go.

"Can we go back to the part where you said you'd do a biker like me?"

"That's not what I said."

"That's what I heard."

"Clean out your ears."

"I need something else cleaned out. Hardly got started last night before you left."

"And you think you're going to get your second shot at me now?"

"No. You're gonna get your second shot at *me* now."

Her head whipped back as she looked up at him. "You think you're irresistible?"

"Never said that."

"That's what I heard," she threw back at him.

He scrubbed his hand across his mouth and when he pulled it away, a smile was there. "You're somethin' else."

"You got that right."

He hesitated and the tip of his tongue came out to run along his bottom lip. Sophie felt that all the way to the apex of her thighs. And when he said, "Wanna kiss you," her gaze rose from his luscious lips back to those blue eyes and she felt herself getting slick.

"You don't always get what you want. Probably learned that in prison," she murmured, dropping her gaze back to his lips as he leaned in.

"I get what I want."

Jesus.

That attitude is what probably landed him behind bars. But, damn, if it didn't make her even wetter.

This was not going well for her. This man could manipulate her simply with his words.

Not. Good.

Though, when he crushed his mouth to hers and slid that skilled tongue of his in between her lips, she decided—

She didn't know what she decided, since she lost all train of thought as he pressed himself against her and the hard, long line of his erection pushed against her belly, as well as that bulky belt buckle.

She dug her fingers into his hair and fisted them. Then pulled back as hard as she could. If she didn't stop this right now, she'd drag him to the floor of her bakery and ride him until she had another couple of unplanned orgasms.

However, no matter how hard she yanked—and she knew his scalp had to be screaming by now—he wouldn't break the kiss. In fact, he deepened it even more.

Pushy.

Cocky.

Trouble with a capital T.

It didn't help that he made her so fucking wet. And once again, she cursed her body when her pussy started to throb.

Throb.

She couldn't ever remember it throbbing solely from a kiss. It had to be the bad boy thing going on, turning her on.

He finally pulled back slightly, his breathing as ragged as hers as he kept his mouth slightly above hers. Probably trying to make a statement that if he wanted to kiss her again, she couldn't do anything to stop it.

"I thought you wanted to keep me safe." She cursed her shaky voice.

"I do."

"But not from you."

"You bein' with me will keep you safe."

"I highly doubt that."

When she finally released her grip on his hair he pulled back farther, his eyes flashing. "You stay in the apartment upstairs?"

He knew about the apartment.

Of course, he would. He was probably born in this town. Lived here all his life, except for doing time. He came to the bakery as a child, for shit's sakes.

So, she couldn't lie. Well, she could, but he'd probably see right through it.

When she didn't answer, he continued, "By yourself."

Uh oh.

He wasn't asking out of concern with her safety. No.

Suddenly her panties were drenched. The thought of him dragging her upstairs, throwing her on her bed and fucking the bejeezus out of her...

Well, yeah, it made her *slightly* wetter. Just slightly.

Damn it.

"Babe, every time I ask you a question an' you don't answer, gonna assume your answer's the one I wanna hear. Got me?"

She opened her mouth but nothing came out.

"Sophie," he said and stepped back.

She caught herself on the display case since, for some reason, her body seemed boneless.

She stared at the reason. Like last night, her conscience warred with itself about whether she should do her best to kick him out and go to bed alone or whether she should stop fighting her body's reaction to the man in black before her.

She bit her bottom lip as she ran her gaze from the top of his head all the way down to the toes of his boots.

"Babe," he said, a warning in his voice.

She shook her head and sucked in a breath. "Tell me what you did to get ten years in prison. I can't be sleeping with a murderer."

He cocked a brow and smothered a smile before answering, "We won't be sleepin', can promise you that."

If he didn't want to answer, the decision would be easy for her. She wanted the truth and nothing but. "Well, that settles it, time for you to go."

His hands planted on his hips and she watched his expression shut down. Suddenly he wasn't so cocky.

His eyes slid from hers before answering, "Anhydrous ammonia."

"What?"

He scrubbed a hand over his bearded chin, avoiding her eyes. "Was accused of stealin' anhydrous ammonia."

She watched him carefully. Words were words. Body language could tell a whole different story. "And did you?"

He frowned, finally meeting her gaze again. "No."

His eyes held hers steadily, not a flicker of anything behind them. She believed him.

"What the hell is it?" Was it used to make explosives?

"Shit used to make meth."

Her brows shot to her hairline. "You make meth?"

His frown deepened into a scowl. "No."

"You ever make meth?"

"No."

"Cops found it on you?"

"My place."

"How much?" Not that she'd know how much was too much, but she was curious and since he was answering, she was asking.

"An ounce or so." Ten years for an ounce. *Or so.* Crazy.

"How'd it get there?"

Sophie watched as his face got hard. A muscled jumped in his jaw. "Not sure."

Now, he *was* lying. He knew. But the thought of whoever placed that chemical in his place made him angry. As it should.

"If you didn't bring it into your own place, someone else did," she stated the obvious.

No answer.

"So, you were set up."

More silence.

"By who?" she prodded.

"Club business, babe." His expression shut down, went blank. Unreadable.

"You went to prison for ten years because you were set up," she tried again.

But, again, he didn't answer. He stared at a spot behind her, not meeting her eyes.

"An ounce of that ammonia stuff put you in jail for ten years."

His nostrils flared. "That an' other stuff."

"What other stuff?"

"My time inside wasn't easy."

"What does that mean?"

His eyes slid to her. "Took no shit."

She couldn't imagine he did. "No time off for good behavior, then."

"No."

"So, you were a bad boy," she whispered.

"Yeah." His eyes cut to her and flashed. "You like to fuck bad boys, babe?"

"Last night was my first time," she admitted.

"Ever?"

"Ever."

"Won't be your last time, though. Guaranteed."

"So you think."

"Don't think," he said with a smile. "Know."

"Cocky."

"Yep."

"Proud of that?"

"Sure."

Sophie laughed, then shook her head. He was a piece of work. And she did not need some badass biker in her life. No, she didn't.

But temporarily in her bed? Maybe. Only for that second round they never got around to.

His eyes cut to the door at the back of the shop that led to the kitchen. "Stairs to the apartment back there?"

"I haven't said yes."

"Don't matter. Your eyes are sayin' it." He stepped closer again, his breath warm against her cheek. "Your nipples are tellin' me, too."

When his thumb brushed against one of those traitorous nipples, she stiffened so she wouldn't arch into his touch.

Damn it. There was no reason to keep fighting the decision she already made, but didn't want to admit to.

She sighed, pinning his hand over her breast with her own. She squeezed it before letting him go. "Follow me."

She pulled away from him and headed toward the swinging door, not even checking to see if he followed. He would. She was sure of it.

"Hold up, babe," he called, and she froze with her hand on the door. He yanked her head back by her ponytail, leaning close enough she could feel his breath along her neck, and slowly slid the elastic band from her hair, letting the messy dark mass fall around her shoulders. "That's better," he whispered.

Sophie looked over her shoulder, pushing her now loose hair away from her face. "Do I have a bruise on my forehead?"

His eyes roamed over her slowly before saying, "Nope."

"'Cause I swear to Christ," she parroted him. "I had to have knocked the sense out of me somehow. Let's go upstairs." She hit the lights to the shop, then slammed the swinging door with her palms and winded her way through the back area towards the private stairway.

His low chuckle behind her shot a shiver down her spine.

"Hurry up," she called back to him and then jogged up the steps.

Chapter Five

ZAK SHOVED his tongue into his cheek as he watched Sophie climb the stairs to her quarters. Nah, more like climbing the stairs to heaven. For him, anyway.

Maybe fate was handing him back the luck he lost when he got convicted of a crime he didn't commit. Throughout his life, there had been plenty of other shit he'd done, but what he went down for wasn't one of them.

Which pissed him off to no end, of course. Ten years living in a tiny cell made of concrete block with what seemed like a different inmate each year could piss you off if you did the crime. Doing time, losing a decade of your life, when you didn't do the crime made you furious.

He pushed the bitterness that clawed at him out of his head as he followed her through the second-floor door to her place. He was relieved to see she had to unlock it first.

She'd be stupid to leave it unlocked when she wasn't up there. Hell, it would be stupid to leave it unlocked even if she was. But then, maybe she was thinking she was stupid by letting him come up to her place, her bedroom... her bed.

No matter what, he'd read in her eyes what she wanted. She couldn't hide it. Though, she probably wasn't a hundred percent happy about it.

He'd do his very best in the next hour to make it one hundred percent.

When she moved over to her small kitchenette to throw her keys on the counter, he went the opposite direction to the windows at the back. He looked down to see a small stone parking lot where her car sat in the dark. No flood lights. That would have to be taken care of. Then he checked the sashes of both windows. Locked. Good. No deck attached for easy access. Good.

The lack of lighting at the rear of the building ate at him though. He turned and was surprised to find her in the middle of the living room, hands on hips, watching him. "You casing the joint?"

"Yeah."

"Thought so. I don't have anything worthwhile to steal."

"You."

"What?"

"You. You're worth stealin'. Some asshole can break in here an' have his way with you against your wishes."

"Like you did last night?"

He shrugged. "You wanted it."

"That's what they all say," she murmured.

There she went again... comparing him to a rapist. Not flattering at all. "Wouldn't have touched you otherwise."

"No, me pounding on your back and screaming, wasn't a sign. At all."

"Some women like it like that."

"Caveman style?"

He shrugged again and his gaze bounced around her apartment. It was small, but still a lot bigger than his room upstairs at the clubhouse. And just as barren. He expected her to have pretty little things strewn about the place. She didn't. Only the basics. Though, nothing wrong with that, either.

"You screamed louder when you came."

She dropped her gaze to her toes, shook her head and then when she finally looked up, she was wearing that sexy smile of hers. Damn, the one that got him in the gut. Naked, wearing that smile, she'd be perfect. And he'd never leave her bed.

"That I did," she finally admitted. "Were you that good when you went in? Or did you learn your techniques in prison? You had lots of time in there to practice."

He liked her sense of humor. He liked her business sense from what he could see so far. He liked her. Period.

But he *loved* sinking into that sweet pussy last night and it was time to get back to business.

Round two. *Ding. Ding. Ding.*

"You're still dressed," he said.

"So are you."

He slipped his cut off his shoulders and placed it with care over an old wooden rocking chair that was within arm's reach. Then crossing his arms in front of him, he grabbed the bottom of his thermal tee and yanked it up over his head, tossing it onto the seat of the same chair.

He bent over, unbuckled his boots and kicked them off, then yanked his socks off by the toes, tossing them to the side.

When he straightened, he was barefoot, bare-chested, just wearing his jeans. He leveled his gaze at her. Her eyes were flashing as she studied his chest full of tattoos.

"More?" he asked.

"Hell yes," she whispered.

He smiled, shook his head and let his fingers drop to his belt buckle. He unclasped it slowly, then unfastened his jeans.

He paused. "Like my tats?"

"No."

"Liar," he said, then pushed his jeans and boxers down his thighs and stepped out of them.

His hard-on bobbed as he stood totally naked about ten feet from her. She was too far away for his liking. And still dressed. Her eyes were glued to his dick, which pulled his balls tight.

"Like my tats now?" he asked, stroking himself slowly.

"Nope," she whispered.

"Get on your knees," he told her. As she rushed forward and

dropped to her knees, he just about fell over in surprise. He did not expect her to do that without some sort of challenge from her first.

When she took him into her mouth, he almost cried. And not cried out, either. Almost shed a fucking tear at how her mouth felt on him. How tight her lips circled him as she rose and fell on his dick. And when she lapped at the crown with her tongue, he dug his hands into her hair and threw his head back.

Holy fuck.

She made a noise at the back of her throat as she took his full length. *Fuckin' A, his whole dick.* The vibrations of that noise just about made him lose it. But he didn't want to lose his load down her throat. Not this time.

He wanted to be inside her when he let loose while listening to her mews, and cries, and demands that he remembered from last night. Noises that were burned into his brain.

"Ah, fuck, babe. Gotta slow down." His voice sounded higher pitched than normal. He cleared his throat. "Holy shit, slow down. I—"

Fuck. He was going to lose it. Like any second now. Her sweet, hot mouth working him made his head spin. When she cupped his balls and squeezed, he jerked back and away from her, breaking the contact.

His chest heaved with his ragged breathing. "I—" He shook his head as he stared down at her, still on her knees looking up at him, her lips shiny, her eyes hooded. "Which door is your bedroom?"

Without a word, she lifted an arm toward an open door. With a growl, he leaned over, hauled her up and over his shoulder in a repeat of last night and strode through the doorway.

"Hit the light," he told her as he paused just inside the room. "Wanna make sure I see your face when you come."

She smacked at the wall and the room lit up. His gaze landed on the bed and in two strides, he had her tossed in the middle. She bounced, gasping.

"Clothes off."

"I—" Now she was the one at a loss for words.

"Clothes off," he repeated. "Hurry."

She scrambled to a seated position and began to pull off her clothes, throwing them to the floor. When she was finally only in her bra and panties he said, "Panties on."

Her eyes shot to him, but she listened. Removing her bra, she tossed it without a care, then stilled.

She wore little pink panties.

"Spread your thighs. Let me see."

She cocked her knees and spread them wide. Just as he thought. Her pink panties were a lot darker along the line of her pussy. Soaked.

She bit her bottom lip. Goddamn, he wanted those teeth in his flesh while he fucked her.

"Tell me you want this. Need to hear it. Don't wanna hear shit 'bout tonight like last night, babe. Not one word that you didn't want this."

"I want this."

"Say it again. Use my name. Wanna make sure there's no mistakin' who's gonna be slidin' deep between your thighs."

"I want this," she repeated on a breath. Her throat bobbed as she swallowed hard and added, "Zak."

He fisted his cock and stroked it once. "That's right, babe. That won't be the only time you're sayin' my name tonight. Guaranteed. Slide those panties off. Hand 'em to me."

Zak's gut clenched as he continued to stroke himself while she did as she was told and held out the damp scrap of cloth to him. He snagged them from her fingers and held them to his nose, inhaling. "Damn, your scent's like honey. Sweet and delicious." He tossed them to the side.

If he remembered later, he'd find them and take them home with him. He wanted to keep a piece of her honeyed goodness with him.

On his knees, he climbed onto the bed between her legs and stared down at her opened to him, both of her hands cupped her tits, and she pinched her own nipples.

Fuck.

Fuck.

Fuck.

He needed to sheath himself deep into her warm, slick cunt, but first... He needed to see if she tasted as good as she smelled. He slid onto his belly and dipped his head, purposely dragging his beard across her tender skin, making her hips jerk. She said something, he had no idea what. And when he did it again, he realized what she was saying, "Fuck me, Zak."

His name on her lips sounded like fucking music to his ears. He would do what he needed to, so he'd hear that favorite song again. And again.

He pressed his lips to her clit and nibbled. Her hips shot off the bed but he went with her, playing with her, teasing, tasting her thoroughly. He sucked the sensitive nub, and she groaned, which in turn, made him groan.

"Fuck me, Zak."

"Soon," he murmured against her flesh, as he slipped two fingers inside her. She was ready. So ready for him.

Him.

Zak Jamison. Felon. Patched member of the DAMC. And at that moment, he didn't think she cared. Right now, to her, he was just Zak. She wanted *him*.

HOLY HELL, she wanted him. *Needed* him now. She pulsed around his fingers, ground against his mouth. She was going to come. Damn. How could anyone be so good with their mouth?

Her hips jerked one more time and then she wrapped her legs around his back as her toes curled, her neck arched, and she screamed out his name. An intense ripple ran through her and her eyes fluttered closed.

When her body finally relaxed and her breathing slowed a little, she dropped her legs back to the bed and tipped her head to look at him. He was still lying between her thighs, peering up her body, a huge smile on his face.

Cocky.

He crawled up her body, his cock sliding along her thigh and when he stopped, the head of it bumped her folds. She opened to him, but he didn't move, just stared down into her eyes and shook his head.

"Got a wrap?"

A what? Oh, fuck.

Fuck.

He didn't come prepared?

"I don't think so."

His brows raised high and he tilted his head as he studied her. "You haven't had anyone in your bed since you moved here?"

"No. I normally don't crawl into bed with just anyone."

"An' you still haven't."

Not just cocky, but damn cocky.

She released a ragged sigh. It still didn't help the situation at hand. "You didn't bring anything in that big-assed wallet of yours?"

"Been a long time since I had to carry around wraps, babe. Not like I needed 'em in prison."

A few thoughts flitted through her mind at his words, but she pushed them away. She didn't think he'd appreciate her bad humor right now. Especially since he had a hard-on that wouldn't quit and no way to relieve it at the moment.

Unless… she finished what she started in the living room. But she wanted him inside her. *Needed* him inside her.

Ugh! Why didn't she buy condoms the last time she went to the grocery store?

Because she never expected to bring a man into her bed. Stupid, but true.

"Now what?" she asked, the disappointment thick in her voice.

"I fuck you."

"Without a condom?"

"Yeah."

"But…"

"Haven't been with anyone in over ten years, babe. Nobody but you an' that was last night. Wasn't with anyone in prison, either, an' that's all I'll say 'bout that. So, yeah, no wrap."

"Uh, I—"

"You on the pill?"

"No."

"*Fuck.*"

"Yeah," she said on a sigh.

He dropped his forehead to hers and blew out a breath. She understood his frustration because she felt it, too.

"Don't need a kid right now," he grumbled.

No shit! She didn't need one, either. Especially with trying to build up her business. Not just that, but one with a felon biker. Even if he'd been falsely accused, he still was labeled a convict. He still had a record.

"Got three options," he started, the crown of his cock sliding along her slick, swollen lips. "One, I run out an' get some. Which might take a little time. Two, you wrap that mouth of yours 'round me like earlier. Promise not to take long if you do. Three, I take your sweet ass. Guess there's a fourth option... We risk it. Up to you, babe. The third option's soundin' pretty good right about now."

The third option? Holy Hannah. That hadn't even crossed her mind. She never let anyone do that before to her. Never planned to, either.

She figured out in her head how long it would take for him to run to the nearest twenty-four-hour convenience store. Or, hell, gas station even. That was probably the smartest option, but—

He continued, "Can tell you I'm not likin' that first option. Might come to your senses an' not let me back in."

True. That could very well happen. Point taken.

"Two would be fine with me, but may not give you what you need."

Another good point.

He dropped his head and sucked one of her nipples deep into his mouth making it pucker. Lightning shot from her nipple to settle in her core. Damn. His cock was right *there*, knocking at her front door. And he wanted to go around to the rear.

"Not sure I wanna risk the last option," he murmured against the curve of her breast, tweaking the other nipple between his fingers. Rolling it, pulling, thumbing the hard tip.

He wasn't making this decision easy for her. No, he wasn't. She closed her eyes, trying to concentrate.

"Can make option three good for both of us." He paused then lifted his head slightly. "Long as you have lube."

That she did have. Mainly because she had this really awesome glass dildo that she used it with. One that hit her G-spot *just* right.

"Not hearin' your vote," he said against her lips before kissing her hard, exploring her mouth with his tongue. Probing, searching, teasing. He swallowed her groan. She swallowed his.

He shoved his face into her neck, inhaling deeply and she shivered. He kissed along her throat. "One?"

He sank his teeth around one nipple and flicked the tip with his tongue. "Two?"

He jackknifed up and flipped her quickly onto her belly before she could protest, nipped the top of her spine, then worked his way down, alternating kisses and bites.

She was going mad. There was nothing more she wanted than him inside her. But no matter how much he was making her lose her mind, she still knew they couldn't risk not using birth control. She was in her prime at thirty-three. And she guessed he was prolific, although she had no idea how old he was. He might be in his early thirties, too.

He grabbed both of her ass cheeks and squeezed, dipping his tongue into her cleft. So close to where he was determined to make his final destination.

"Three?" And then he licked her *there*. Just a teasing touch with the tip of his tongue. Once more. Then he was gone.

Sophie turned her head to watch him as he ripped open her nightstand drawer, digging. He made a noise at the back of his throat, then smiled wide. His eyes flicked to her, then back into the drawer.

Yeah, he found her stash.

He not only took out the tube of lube she had, but two of her vibrators, the larger one was latex, the smaller one plastic. He studied each one, turned them on, tested the strength of the vibrations against his palm, then shut them back off. He lifted his head to look at her again.

"Gonna be even better than I thought," he said, moving back to settle between her legs.

He kissed each cheek, then grabbed a mouthful of her flesh between his teeth and shook it gently with a growl. Just enough to get her juices flowing again. The tip of his finger stroked between her quivering cheeks, blazing a path down, down, *down,* pausing to gather some of her slickness before moving back up to where he started.

He did it again.

And once more.

He was determined to drive her to the edge. And she would go with free will. That was for sure.

Something wet and warm touched her back *there* again, probed, teased, and she relaxed as much as she could. His tongue was replaced quickly with a roaming finger, doing the same thing.

When she heard a snap of the cap on the lube, she swallowed hard, her lips parting as her breathing shallowed. The cool gel was a shock against her heated skin, a total contrast to the warmth of his tongue and finger.

Then he was pushing gently, slowly. "That's it, babe. Take me. Give this to me. Give me everything. All of you. Let me make this mine." Her body melted into the bed at his murmurs, his whispers, his attempt at calming her spinning mind.

When she brought him upstairs, this was not what she had planned. But the sensations were nothing like she ever felt before. So unexpected. So crazy good. He slipped one knuckle deep, then two. Coaxing her gently, murmuring against her back as he did it.

"Don't know if this is gonna work, babe. So fuckin' tight. Might have to run out an'—"

"No... Don't go. Stay, keep going."

"Fuck, babe. *Fuck*. You're gonna be the death of me. Survived ten years in the joint to be released an' die happy inside you. That'd be the way to go."

Sophie smiled into her folded arms, but it quickly disappeared when he worked her faster.

Suddenly, he slipped from her and she felt empty.

He slapped her ass lightly. "Up. On your knees. Keep your pretty head down." God, they needed condoms and he needed to fuck her... like now!

He had iron-clad control, because he didn't fuck her, instead she heard the hum of a vibrator. Her small purple one; she recognized the sound of it easily.

"Gonna get you so that you're fuckin' beggin' me, babe. No doubt."

His tone didn't sound so cocky now. The way his soft words slipped from his lips, they sounded caring. He wanted to make sure she was ready for him.

The pressure of the small vibrator against the tight rim of her ass made her clench, then as the pulsations radiated through her, she relaxed. Opened to him. Invited him to do whatever he intended.

He hooked an arm around her hips, reaching beneath her to press a thumb against her clit, circling, rubbing, and she opened up even more for him.

"That's it, babe," he murmured, the smooth, lubed vibrator sinking deeply, easily into her.

Her eyelids fluttered and eyes rolled back.

Holy hell, if she knew it felt like this, she would have done this a long time ago.

"You fuckin' like that," he said, his voice low, strained. He had to be suffering at this point, his erection thick against her thigh.

He began to fuck her with the dildo, while playing with her clit until she cried out, her body convulsing uncontrollably. But he didn't stop, no, he continued until she lost her mind, desperate for him now. Dying for him to be inside her, to take her completely. And she didn't care where. Somewhere. Anywhere.

Soon.

"Zak," she groaned.

"Soon, babe," he promised. "Can't wait much longer, either."

"Zak," she called again, her voice breathless.

"Gotta make sure—"

"Zak," she wailed, dragging his name out until she ran out of breath.

"Fuck," he muttered.

"Oh, God, Zak."

"Goddamn it," he muttered some more.

"Oh, holy... *Fuck,*" she cried out.

He released a hiss, slipped the vibrator from her, shut it off, then she heard the larger one.

Damn, she couldn't take another one. She wanted him inside her instead. Not a toy. Him. Real. Hard. All male.

But he pressed the larger vibrator to her clit first, making her jump because it was now so sensitive. Then he slid it back and slipped it easily between her soaked folds. Her back arched as he seated it deep and held it still.

Her head rolled from side to side as she called his name again.

He cursed. And suddenly, he was there, the smooth slick head of his cock gliding against her, asking her permission to enter.

He pressed harder, struggling to get past the tight ring without hurting her. And it did hurt. Though, not enough to tell him to stop. She wanted him to hurry, become a part of her. Take her to the ends of the Earth and back.

Badass biker. Ex-con. Forbidden sex. A thrill ran through her. She gasped when he pushed further, farther, taking it home. Stretching her, filling her. Making her his.

Being the first, and maybe the only one, to take her there.

With both the vibrations radiating from her core and him settled deep inside her ass, she bit her lip, her body, her mind spinning out of control.

She wanted him to move, but he didn't. He remained still, quiet. But she could hear his breath, his deep, but rapid rasping. He started to speak, but his words dissipated into thin air. He tried again, but she couldn't catch any of those words, either.

She found herself on another plane, another level. Honestly, she didn't care what he had to say, only cared about what he was about to do.

And when he did it, she cried out. He was right, she would beg him. Beg him for more. Beg him to go faster. Beg him to go deeper.

"Okay?"

Even when her lips parted to answer him, assure him she was all right, nothing came out. Nothing but a lost breath escaped.

He folded over her, gripped her hair and pulled her head back, arching her neck. His lips found her ear. "Fuckin' can't hold on, babe. Can't. Sorry."

It didn't matter, her body decided she couldn't, either. She tensed around his cock and the vibrator, both deep inside her, as the waves crashed through her, sweeping her under, dragging him along for the ride.

He barked out a curse and sank his teeth into her shoulder, tensing against her, pinning his hips to hers, his cock pulsating within her. His hot breath beat rapidly against the skin of her neck. When it started to slow, he lifted some of his weight off her. The vibrator slipped from her, the hum becoming silent.

She waited for him to pull out, but he didn't. He stayed connected, grasping her hips tightly, then leaning over to brush a line of kisses down her spine.

Something she never expected a badass biker would do. Never expected him to be... tender.

"Give me a few, babe. Don't wanna pull out 'til I'm softer."

Caring.

Shit.

She needed him to be hard, uncaring, just worried about getting his rocks off. She needed him to make it easy to kick him out of her apartment, out of her life, once they were done. Not make her wonder what it would be like if he was a part of her life, hell, in her bed, on a regular basis.

Because that couldn't happen. She didn't need the complications of a man with not only a caveman mentality, but one who might scare away customers from her fledgling business. She didn't need ties to a local motorcycle club and all the headaches that most likely went along with it. And who knew what type of illegal activities they were involved in.

She didn't know much about the biker life, nor did she have any plans to find out.

He carefully slipped from her and rolled off the bed. "Where's the can?"

"Can?"

"Room with the shitter, sink, an' shower?"

Ah. The *can*. The bathroom.

She waved her arm toward the open bedroom door and slid onto her belly with a sigh. "Next door over." She wiggled her hips, testing to see if there was any pain or discomfort.

A little.

She had a feeling she might feel it more in the morning.

"Don't move."

She turned her face on the pillow and watched as he walked his muscular, *not tattooed*, naked ass out of her room.

She wondered if he'd keep going, get dressed and walk out the door. It would be for the best. But then, he wouldn't have given her a caveman order, would he have? No.

With such thin walls in the apartment, she heard the toilet flush, the sink running for a few moments, and him talking to himself.

She couldn't quite make out what he was saying, but he was having a full-blown conversation and she doubted he had his cell phone with him. He was definitely talking to himself.

She giggled, but cut it off quickly when he walked back into the room carrying a washcloth.

She raised her eyebrows at him when he stopped at the side of the bed, studying her. Then he climbed on and gently cleaned her up.

Gently. Cleaned. Her. Up.

He couldn't do this to her. It was unfair. He was cheating. Though, what he was cheating at she didn't want to know. She just knew her heart squeezed and then thumped as he took care of her.

Damn it.

Was he really a biker? Did bikers do these types of things?

Her eyes followed the damp washcloth as he threw it onto the floor.

Yeah. There it was. A good reminder he was a Neanderthal.

She sighed and rolled over between his legs so he straddled her thighs, looking down at her.

"Your tits are as sweet as your ass."

Well, there it was. Another good reminder. So romantic.

"I'm glad you approve," she returned, then propped two pillows under her head to let her gaze roam over his body. From hips to neck, the man was almost solid tattoos. The front covered in different sizes, different colors. The back, she noticed on his trip to the bathroom, was done in black and gray. And what was permanently inked into the skin of his broad, muscular back was a mirror of the patches that were sewn onto the back of the leather vest he wore.

"You must be loyal to your club to tattoo that whole thing on your back."

He sucked in a deep breath and his chest expanded. His sense of pride was unmistakable.

"Loyalty is to the brotherhood. Family."

"Brotherhood," she repeated.

"Yeah."

She wanted to ask about his real family, but that meant she'd become more invested in him. And she should avoid that. She had to steel her heart. She didn't want sex to become intimacy.

That could—*would*—be trouble.

He dropped forward, grabbing both of her wrists and pinning them to the bed above her head.

She tugged slightly to see how tightly he held her. He didn't release or let up even a bit.

"Next time, want your teeth in me."

She frowned. "What does that mean?"

His eyes flashed, his expression hungry again. Like earlier. Like last night.

"Your teeth." He curled his upper lip like a snarling dog before pressing his mouth to her shoulder. "In me." He sank those straight, white teeth into her flesh.

Damn.

Every nerve ending suddenly came alive. Easy to understand why he wanted that. But...

"Got that part," she struggled to get out. "I was wondering more about the 'next time.'"

He licked the spot where he bit her, shrugged, then flopped onto his back next to her, his left arm folded above his head. "Next time."

Clearly, he was mistaken that there would be a next time. No reason to point out how wrong he was.

Instead, she said, "You're not big on conversation, apparently."

"I converse."

"Two word answers don't make a conversation."

He rolled onto his side, his head propped on one hand, the other traveling along her ribs. "Chicks need that shit. All that extra crap. No point in all that. Say what you mean."

"Why not just grunt and pound your chest? Apparently, that used to work, too."

"You need a bigger bed."

Sophie shook her head at the change in subject. "It's perfectly fine for me."

"Tight for us."

"There's no us."

"I like this."

Holy shit, she was going to pry his damn mouth open and pull out complete sentences if it was the last thing she did.

"This?"

He waved a hand above the bed, above the two of them. "This."

"You haven't had sex in ten years, of course you're going to like it."

"That's not it."

"That's all it is. Nothing more."

"Nope."

She wasn't going to argue. Her eyes tipped toward the digital clock on her nightstand. It was creeping up on eleven o'clock.

She shifted and then groaned at the sudden soreness in her backside.

"You okay?"

"Fine." She pushed herself up to her elbows, then up to a seat, trying to hide her wince. "I have to get some sleep. I need to get up early to get some baking done before the shop opens."

He jerked his shoulders. "So sleep."

"Zak."

"Babe."

"Zak, you have to go. *This,"* she circled her hand over them, "isn't a thing."

"It's a thing."

"You just got out of jail. You need to get back to living your life."

"I'll go back to that. Don't mean you won't be a part of it."

She sighed and scrubbed a hand across her eyes. He wasn't making any move to leave her bed.

"You gotta go," she told him again.

"I'll go in the morning." He snagged her around the waist and pulled her to him, curving his chest to her back. "I'll pick up some wraps for tomorrow night."

"Tomorrow night?" she squeaked.

"Yeah, party at church, then we can head upstairs after or head back here. Your choice."

That didn't seem like much of a choice.

"Don't wear anything too revealin' to the party. No tits hangin' out for everyone to see. They're mine."

They're his? What bizarro world had she fallen into? All because she was desperate for money and made a freaking cake for a motorcycle gang... or club. Whatever! She should've gone with her gut and said no.

She had to admit, though, those couple hundred dollar bills stashed in her cash register downstairs would help immensely.

She tried to slide out of his arms and he snaked them tighter around her, nuzzling his nose in her hair.

"Okay. First of all... Hell, I don't even know where to start." She growled in frustration. "Okay, first, let's get something straight. I'm not yours. My *tits* aren't yours. I'm not going to any party with you. Especially at a *church!* And we're not doing this again."

"Pickin' you up at eight."

She couldn't stop the laughter that bubbled up. She couldn't help it. This whole thing was so absurd!

"Either you're crazy or I'm crazy." The laughter turned into a hiccup, then suddenly tears were sliding down her cheeks. She sniffled and wiped at them.

His arm loosened, and he rolled her onto her back. His eyebrows knitted together as he thumbed a tear from the corner of her eye. "Babe. Why you cryin'?"

Why was she crying? It wasn't obvious? Well, maybe it wasn't. Maybe she had been giving him mixed signals. Maybe he needed some clarification.

She felt the hysteria rise from her chest into her voice. "Why? Because I don't want you here. I don't want you in my apartment. I don't want you in my bed."

He stilled then. His body got hard, tight. "Got it. I'm not good enough." He pushed himself up and put some space between them.

He rolled to his feet and stood up. He jerked a hand toward her. "I get it. You're good. I'm not." He tapped a finger to his temple. "Got it. Won't forget it."

It wasn't—

Well, that might be a small part of it.

But that wasn't all it was. "I don't even know you. Minutes after first laying eyes on you, I'm not only in your bed but you're in *me*. Not even twenty-four hours later, you're in my ass!" She couldn't control the shrill rise in her words.

"You liked it."

She sat up abruptly, her eyebrows shooting to her hairline. "It's not about liking it. It's... It's... *Fuck*!" she shouted, slamming her palm on the mattress, pissed she couldn't put her mixed feelings into words, make him understand.

Bottom line was, how could she make him understand when she

didn't even understand it herself, couldn't process the confusion that was the last twenty-four hours.

He dropped his hands to his hips and grinned. "You're cute when you're mad."

She reached for one of the discarded vibrators and chucked it at him. Instead of thumping him in the head like she wanted it to, he ducked and it smacked the wall behind him with a thud. If she broke one of her favorite toys, she'd be even madder at him.

When he straightened, he shook his head, his smile now gone.

Good. Because she wasn't finding this amusing and he shouldn't either. "You can leave now."

His nostrils flared and so did his eyes. Between gritted teeth, he said, "You got it, babe."

With relief, and maybe a touch of surprise that he was finally actually listening to her, she watched him turn and head his too-fine nakedness out of her bedroom door, while he muttered, "Swear to Christ, you're gonna be wearin' my cut before you kill me."

Her hands flew up in frustration at the unfamiliar language he used. "What does that mean?"

She needed a damn Biker to English dictionary.

The door slamming was her answer.

She pushed down the regret that fought to replace her short-lived relief.

Chapter Six

HAWK, with both palms planted on the bar, leaned towards Zak. "You comin' to work for me?"

Zak studied the tall, massively muscular man before him. He reminded himself to never be on the man's bad side. Or Hawk's brother's bad side, either, since Diesel was just as big, though much *badder.* They were built similarly like their father Ace, but they both outweighed their old man and all that weight was solid *don't-fuck-with-me* badassery.

At six feet, Zak was no small man, and he'd had plenty of time in prison to work on his body, building up muscle he never had before. But no matter how often or how much weight he pumped, he would never be Hawk or Diesel big. That shit was in their genes.

Grizz grumbled on the stool next to him, nursing a beer. "Man don't wanna work in a fuckin' bar. He can't work behind the bar, 'cause you need women who look good back there to attract customers. Like Bella does. An' he ain't gonna be no damn line cook in the kitchen. Or a dishwasher."

"Did plenty of that shit in prison. Not lookin' to continue that career path," Zak muttered.

"Right," Grizz continued. "Plus, Mama helps cook for the parties anyhow. With the line cooks you already got, Hawk, you're set in the kitchen."

Mama Bear's gray-haired head popped out of the swinging doors from the shared commercial kitchen that separated the club's private bar and The Iron Horse. "You need me, old man?" she asked her husband.

His wrinkled face frowned, deepening those crevices, and he swatted a hand in the direction of his wife. "No. Did I call you, woman? Get back in the kitchen."

Zak bit back his smile. Grizzly was one of the first patched members of the club after its inception. He and Mama Bear were like grandparents to Zak. Hell, like grandparents to everyone. The older man hardly rode his Harley anymore due to his arthritis, his bursitis, and every other "*itis*" he had. Even so, he was still an entrenched member of the club and would be until the day he died. Then they'd fill his Harley's gas tank with his ashes so they could display them on the mantel behind the bar, right next to Bear's.

"Crotchety old fuck," Mama griped loud enough to make sure they all heard her and ducked back into the kitchen. She was busy cooking and directing the line cooks to make the food for tonight's party.

No matter how much they grumbled and bitched at each other, everyone knew the couple loved each other to death. No one questioned that. Seemed like they'd been married since the beginning of time. And Zak knew that when one finally succumbed to the motorcycle club in the sky, the other would shortly follow. They were never far apart in life, he doubted they would be in death.

That was true love. True companionship. True loyalty.

Something he envied and hoped to find for himself one day.

Throughout the club's history, some of the brothers cheated on their ol' ladies. If another brother caught them, they kept it to themselves. Didn't mean they approved, but the brotherhood was strong enough not to rat each other out. Eventually, most of them got caught and life became a living hell for them. Rule was, don't piss in your ol' lady's Cheerios unless you wanted to turn into a dead man walking.

Life became so miserable until she either left your cheating ass or she forgave you. The first was quicker than the second.

"All right, brother," Hawk continued. "Then what're you goin' to do?"

A bakery with a woman that tasted honey sweet popped into his mind. But he wasn't going to share that with his brothers just yet. A bakery might not be a typical club business, but it was a solid business nonetheless.

"Might have somethin' in mind that I'm keepin' on the D.L."

Hawk cocked a brow. "You got somethin' on the down low? You talkin' a new venture?"

"Yeah, maybe. If it don't pan out, then I'll find somethin'. Run a wrecker for Rig. Or help D out with the security biz. Speaking of, need to talk to him about cameras, lighting, an' a security system."

"For?"

Zak cocked a brow his direction.

"Never mind. Gotcha, brother. It's on the D.L." Hawk's eyes lifted and he frowned over Zak's shoulder. "Ah, shit. Here comes trouble."

Zak turned to follow Hawk's gaze at the same time a few groans and soft whistles rose up from some of the hang-arounds and prospects who were playing pool and getting an early start on their partying.

Zak blinked to clear his vision, then his eyes narrowed as he watched the gorgeous woman—clearly no longer a girl—sashay her way across the clubhouse. No question on a direct path to where he and Hawk were.

Holy fuck.

Next to him, Grizz grumbled, "Goddamn it," and slammed his pint glass down on the wooden bar top.

She tossed her long dark brown hair as if she knew she was being watched—because she certainly was—but ignored everyone else, only having eyes for Zak as she approached. Her baby blues flashed, and a smile crossed her face.

Jayde was a woman on a mission. A determined woman could be a dangerous one.

Though, when she got to him, he couldn't miss the shine of tears in her eyes. His nostrils flared as he fought his own. He cleared his throat, then echoed Grizz. "Goddamn it."

When she was within arm's reach, he wrapped a hand around the back of her neck and hauled her close, shoving his nose into her hair and inhaling her scent. Jayde's arms circled his waist and squeezed him tight. Her body hiccupped against him.

He released her, shoved her back slightly, then cupped her cheeks, staring down into her tear-streaked face. He wiped at her cheeks with his thumbs, whispered, "Fuckin' Jayde," then placed a kiss on her forehead.

Her lips trembled, but the first thing tumbling out of her mouth was, "Dad and Axel don't know I'm here."

Zak shook his head. "Can't imagine they do."

"I'm supposed to stay away from the club."

Yeah, their father and brother didn't want his little sister anywhere near the club, involved in its business or its brothers. Or anywhere near him.

Bad influence.

"Mom know?"

Jayde blinked clear a few more tears as she said, "Yeah. She misses you, Z."

Zak flattened his lips and steeled himself. He missed his mother, too. Both Jayde and his mother. But his mother wasn't going to go against the word of his father. She couldn't do that and keep peace in their family, or their marriage.

Zak understood. He didn't like it. It pained him. But he understood.

"You shouldn't be here, girly," Grizz barked. Pushing himself off the stool, looking grumpy as all fuck, he came over to push Zak out of the way so he could envelope Jayde in his arms and kiss her on the top of her head.

"Hey, Grizz." Her voice was muffled in his barrel-like chest.

"Hey, yourself. You been good?" He held her an arm's length away to take a long look at her. "You look good. All grown up." He glanced toward Hawk. "See? This is what you need behind the bar, not an ugly puss like Z."

"Right," Hawk scoffed. "Just what I need, two fuckin' pissed-off cops huntin' me down. Then havin' the PD targetin' the bar. Just what we *all* need."

"My sister will never work behind the bar," Zak assured Hawk. "Even if she *was* part of the club."

"You got that right," Hawk grumbled. "Wanna pop?" he asked her.

Jayde smiled at him. "You know I'm more than old enough to drink now, Hawk."

"Really?"

"Yeah, I'm twenty-four, now. Not a little girl."

"You'll always be a little girl to us," Grizz grumbled. His eyes slid to the right and Zak followed the old man's gaze to Squirrel. The younger prospect had his eyes locked on Jayde and was heading their direction.

"Go sit your ass down somewhere, Squirrel," Grizz shouted his warning. "Don't embarrass yourself by havin' this old man kick your ass in front of everyone. None of you wet-behind-the-ears assholes better come anywhere near this girl."

Squirrel slid to a stop with his eyes wide at Grizz's words before spinning on his heel, then heading back the direction he came.

"Smart move, squirrel dick," Hawk yelled out.

Laughter rose from the group of younger guys hanging around one of the pool tables and when Squirrel rejoined them, they took turns shoving him in jest.

"Those shitters better be sparklin' clean for the party tonight. Got me?" Hawk warned them.

"They're good, Hawk," one voice reassured him.

"Better be. Or else you'll all be outside lookin' in with your dicks in your hands."

The voices in the room dropped to a low murmur, and the group went back to playing pool to stay off Hawk's radar.

Zak didn't miss Jayde's gaze lingering on Abe, one of the newer prospects. Zak didn't know much about him, since today was the first time he met the younger guy, but from what he saw, he seemed decent, put together. But that didn't matter.

"Don't even think about it," Zak said.

Jayde turned to face him, color in her cheeks. "What? I would be skinned alive. You know that."

"Yeah, I do. So, when you're in this club, put your blinders on. You hear?"

"You having a party tonight?"

"Yeah, an' you won't be here."

Grizz and Hawk both nodded in agreement.

Jayde looked up at him and said, "You don't have to be here, either. You can walk away. Come home."

Out of the corner of his eye, he noticed Hawk straighten and stiffen, while Grizz shook his head and sat back on his bar stool to stare down at his beer, wearing a frown.

Zak wrapped his fingers around Jayde's bicep, pulled her around the bar and into the meeting room next to it, shutting the door behind him.

"Repeat what you just said," Zak growled. He loved his sister. Hell, he missed his sister. Hadn't seen her since she was fourteen and was just a gangly teen. But she knew how important this club was to him. So, it surprised him when she said what she did.

Jayde spread her booted feet, crossed her arms over her chest, and looked him directly in the eye. "I said you can walk away. Come home."

Yeah, she was a fucking Jamison all right. Stubborn, proud, and not afraid of shit. And this club was just as much in her blood as it was his. Only their parents wanted her to have a blood transfusion and rid her of any desire to be a part of the life.

He leaned back against the heavy wood meeting table that practically filled the room. He crossed his arms and ankles, and studied the girl-turned-woman before him.

He couldn't say he disagreed with them. His sister was a college graduate. She was smart. She could make something of herself and go far in life. Hell, leave Shadow Valley in her rearview mirror. She didn't need to get bogged down with bikers and the club life. Though, certain women were respected and revered, they didn't hold any power in this game. She deserved better than that.

He dragged a hand through his too-long hair. "Can't. You know that. They're family."

It wasn't that he couldn't. He wouldn't.

"No, Zak. *We're* family. And I need my big brother."

It pained Zak to swallow down the lump in his throat.

While he was down, she went for the jugular. "You want to end up back behind bars?"

His heart skipped a beat. "Not gonna happen."

"It might. This club may be your downfall. You know the motto... Down and dirty 'til dead."

Was she mocking their motto?

"No, things are different. Gonna do my best to make it better."

"It's a fucking motorcycle club, Z. Full of badass bikers, not that I need to tell you that. No matter how much you clean up this club, it's going to have a stink. That's why Dad didn't want a part of it. Nor did Axel."

Zak studied his sister, wiser than her years. "You shouldn't be here," he finally said.

"I'm not here," she stated with a poker face.

"Let's keep it that way. Go home, Jayde." If word got back to Mitch or Axel that Jayde had been here, it could bring a world of shit down on them. They didn't need it.

He didn't need it.

"Mom wants to see you."

Zak's eyebrows shot up his forehead and he shifted his feet. "Yeah?"

"Yeah, but in secret."

His excitement quickly turned to disappointment. "Right." He pushed off the table to his feet, then headed toward the door.

"She wants me to set something up."

Zak hesitated. "When?"

Jayde came up next to him and shrugged before yanking open the door. "Give me your cell and I'll make sure she gets it."

"Give me your phone." When she did, Zak plugged his number into her contacts. "Make sure Dad doesn't go through your phone."

"Oh hell no. You forget I'm twenty-four not fourteen. I keep it locked at all times unless it's in my hand."

Zak eyeballed his sister. He wasn't sure if her hiding stuff from their father was good or bad. Made him worry a bit that she may be doing things she shouldn't be.

She walked out of the meeting room and he trailed behind her to make sure she left and left without any of the horny younger guys bothering her.

"Sure I can't come to the party tonight?" she tossed over her shoulder.

"Fuck no. An' don't even try to sneak in."

When she said, "Okay," too quickly, Zak's eyes narrowed.

"That flip answer just got me puttin' the word out to keep an eye peeled for you. Anyone spots you they'll come to me. Don't let that happen."

"Whatever."

Zak gritted his teeth as he pushed the back door open and guided her out. "I'm serious, Jayde."

"I hear you," she answered, a smile pulling at her lips.

"Fuck," he muttered then scanned the parking lot. "Which one's yours?"

Jayde shot a hand toward a newer yellow Chevy Camaro SS. It was a beautiful piece of machinery, even if it wasn't a bike, and he wondered how she could afford it.

"How'd you get that?"

"Dad."

Well, there it was. She couldn't afford it. "Really?"

"Yeah. Graduation present."

Zak shook his head. "Damn."

"Sweet, right?"

It sure fucking was. He glanced at the old junker Crash lent him. It wasn't parked far from her car. He couldn't pick Sophie up in that piece of shit. She already didn't think he was good enough for her.

And he probably wasn't.

Fucking damn.

He needed to do something about his ride. At least until the weather was a little warmer and he could get his bike out of storage and back in tip-top condition. Then her ass will be on the back with that thick hair of hers blowing in the wind.

"Jealous?" his sister asked with a smile.

"Hell yes." No point in lying.

"Come home. Maybe Dad will buy you a car."

He snorted. "Jayde. I'm not comin' home. I'm fuckin' thirty-two years old."

"Yeah, well, sucks to be you then."

Zak laughed and shook his head. "Now, get gone." He leaned over and planted a kiss on her cheek, then gave her a gentle shove towards her sweet ride. "Love ya, Jayde."

"Love you, too, Z."

"Don't wanna see your ass here again," he called as she swung open her car door.

"Okay," she called back as she ducked into the driver's seat.

That easy "okay" also worried him.

He waited until she drove out of the lot before heading back inside. He stopped inside the door, stuck two fingers in his mouth and whistled loudly. All heads turned his way. "No one touches that. Hear me? No. One. You see her 'round this club, you find me immediately. Got me?"

A few "Got you's" answered him. His eyes found Abe and the other man gave him a chin lift. Zak frowned.

Fuck.

Chapter Seven

SOPHIE HAD no idea what happened to her life. One minute she's totally focused on building her bakery business, and the next?

She closed her eyes and groaned. Somehow the next, she's being pulled through a crowd of rowdy bikers and their "bitches" in the cold night air, heading toward a roaring bonfire that appeared to be made up of a mountain of wood pallets. The flames licked halfway to heaven.

As Zak strode forward, Sophie leaned back trying to slow him down a bit. She was wearing her very favorite suede knee-high boots. The brown ones that had a really nice heel on them that made her legs look longer. And slimmer. Because that was important, too. However, the heel didn't make it easy to walk in the dark over stones, dead grass and rough patches of dirt.

She had a feeling she would end up on her ass. She should have worn sneakers instead.

Especially since she wasn't trying to impress anyone here.

She didn't even want to be here in the first place.

How the hell did she even end up here tonight?

The man currently hauling her around left pissed off last night and she had no clue why he even insisted on pursuing her… pursuing this. Whatever the hell *this* was.

The worst part was she had shut down the bakery early, locked the door, turned off all the lights, and went upstairs to hide just in case he *did* show up at eight. Like he had threatened.

And when 8:05 came around and he hadn't shown up, she had breathed a sigh of relief. But then, she should have realized that bikers probably weren't prompt or watched the time. Life apparently revolved around them, not the clock.

Nope, fuck everyone else.

So, she left the lights off in her apartment, too, and wearing a pair of yoga pants and an old, soft sweatshirt, she sank onto her couch to catch up on some TV.

Well, that was until there was a man in black standing before her, hands on his hips.

And if that didn't make her scream and her heart beat a million miles a minute, nothing would.

She had no idea how he got in or why she didn't hear him. Maybe he was right about the shop needing better security.

She needed it just to keep him out.

But as he stood over her, her stomach dropped—once it stopped spinning. Holy Hannah, even in the glow of the TV he looked good with his badass clothes, his badass tats, and his badass bod.

He jerked his stubbled chin in her direction. "That what you're wearin'?"

"How did you get in here?"

"Told you I'd be here at eight."

She raised her eyebrows in disbelief. "I locked the door."

"Know it. Diesel will be makin' your place more secure."

He knew someone named after fuel. Okay, then.

"Question was: That what you're wearin'?"

She looked down at her clothes, then back up at him. *He* was judging *her* clothing choices? "Uh, no. I'm not going."

He blinked slowly as if trying to keep his patience. "Babe."

Maybe he should be more worried about *her* patience. "My name is Sophie."

"Know what your name is."

"Babe is a pig in a movie."

She swore she heard him snort. Though, it sounded much sexier than a pig.

"Got wraps. We can stay here an' fuck, or we can go to church."

Sophie heard the silent, "And then fuck," he was tacking onto the end of that in his mind.

Wasn't much of a choice. "How about neither. I hate church."

This time he definitely snorted. He leaned over and switched on the lamp next to the couch. Sophie squinted as her eyes adjusted to the light.

Hot damn, he looked even better in the light.

Fuck her life.

His beard was freshly trimmed tight to his jaw, his hair actually looked like he ran a comb through it even though it had a shaggy, sexy tousled look to it. His eyes were lit up with amusement.

Then there was the rest of him. He had a well-fitting pair of Levi's encasing his long legs which ended at his black biker boots, of course. And on her way back up, she noticed the same belt as yesterday, and couldn't forget that grimy black leather vest. Under it was a black thermal Henley that snugged his torso. And his muscular arms. And that muscular chest of his. She finally let her eyes rise to his and he wore a wide smile.

Cocky.

"Babe. Yeah, thinkin' stayin' here an' fuckin' may be the choice you'll be makin'. I brought a few."

Sophie shook herself out of her daze. "A few what?"

"Wraps. Nothin's gonna hold us back tonight."

Well, that was a relief.

Not.

Goddamn it.

So, now, here she was getting her ass planted in front of the bonfire with his arm hanging heavily around her neck like a noose. If that wasn't bad enough, she couldn't miss that she was getting the eyeball from some of the other women and definitely from some of the men.

It wasn't because her tits were hanging out. Oh, no. He had pulled her from the couch into her bedroom and had picked out what she was going to wear. What she was *allowed* to wear.

Cocky.

A thick, high-necked sweater, which, in her opinion, made her breasts look even bigger, and a pair of hip-hugging jeans tucked into her boots. Then he had said, "Need to get you a vest."

"Why? Is it going to be that cold?" she'd asked.

To that he just shook his head and hauled her out of her apartment after making sure all the doors were locked, tucking her into the passenger seat of a car she was surprised he drove. Mainly because it was such a clunker.

Then he flipped his vest inside out before getting in the driver seat. When she gave him a questioning look, he ignored her, blaring the radio and driving like a madman through the streets of Shadow Valley and into the private parking lot behind The Iron Horse.

Presently, she tried to ignore the looks being shot her way. "So, what's the party for tonight?"

"It's Saturday night."

"I know. So, what's the party for tonight?"

Zak tugged her closer, a beer hanging from the fingers in one hand, his eyes crinkling at the corners. "You're cute."

"So… what I'm getting is that there isn't any reason for this party, other than it's Saturday night."

He lifted the bottle to his lips. "Yep." Sophie watched his throat move as he swallowed.

Goddamn it.

To distract herself from all that was hot, fuckable Zak, she continued to chatter. "You guys just had a party a couple nights ago."

"Pig roast. Different."

"What the hell's the difference between a pig roast and a party?"

"A pig."

Sophie threw her hands up and groaned. For her sanity, she decided to broach another subject. "Who are these women? Some sort of groupies?"

Zak grinned. "Somethin' like that. Some are ol' ladies. Some *not*. Some are strippers from Heaven's Angels. They like to hang with us."

She ignored the stripper part since she'd been rudely introduced to three of them the other night while in Zak's bed. His homecoming offering from a dude named Dawg. How fitting. And disturbing.

"Ol' ladies?"

"Yeah, they belong to a brother."

"Like a wife?"

"Some are." He tipped his bottle towards one of the women walking away from the fire. The flames cast a glow onto the back of her vest. "See what she's wearin'?"

The woman wore a vest that had three patches very clearly declaring her, "Property of Pierce," in large capital letters on her back. No missing that.

That had better not be the type of vest Zak mentioned earlier about her wearing. There was no way she'd ever wear something that declared her property of a man. Any man.

No way, no how.

As Sophie's eyes surveyed the crowd, she noticed not too many of the women wore them. That was a relief.

"What's the difference between being an ol' lady and not being one?"

"A whole lot."

"Like?"

"Like you belong to your man."

Sophie rolled her eyes. She never heard anything so archaic. "And the rest of the women don't belong to anyone."

"Nope."

"Fair game."

"Yep. Here to entertain us. Please us. Serve us. Whatever."

Entertain them. Please them. Serve them. *Whatever*. Sophie pulled away enough to stare up at him. "You can just pick any one of them and fuck them?"

"One. Two. More."

"More," Sophie echoed, eyes narrowed. More caveman shit.

"They wanna hang 'round the club, hang 'round us, they need to make it worth our while. They drink our booze, eat our food, then they get our dick. They clean church. They help cook sometimes. Small price to pay."

Sophie arched an eyebrow. "Really." She didn't understand the thrill of hanging out with a bunch of Neanderthals on the chance of ending up in one of their beds temporarily. As if they were sex gods. Which she was sure most of them were not.

A shocking thought made her ask in a shaky whisper, "Am I one of them?"

Zak turned to her, slid a thumb down her cheek, then cupped her chin to raise her face to his. "No, babe, you're not."

"What makes me different?"

His eyes shuttered, and he hesitated. "'Cause you're mine."

"What do you mean I'm yours?"

"Mine. Self-explanatory."

"Am I your ol' lady?" she asked, struggling to keep the panic out of her voice.

"Not yet. But you will be."

"So goddamned cocky."

"Don't see you fightin' it."

"Can't fight what doesn't exist."

"It exists."

Sophie sighed. He had to be one of the most frustrating men she ever met.

"You'll accept it."

And there it was. Grunt. Grunt. Pound. Pound. Club a woman, then drag her around by her hair.

"Are you all like this?"

He took another swig of his beer, then dropped his eyes to her. "Like what?"

"Like you."

"Doubt it."

"Thank fuck for that," she murmured.

He laughed and pressed his lips to her temple. "Sophie, look at me."

Why she did, she'll never know. Maybe it was the way he said it, his voice low in her ear, sexy, drawing a response from deep within her belly. But fool that she was, she looked up.

Then his lips came down. He took ownership of her mouth right there in front of the fire, in front of his friends, his buddies, and all the females that had been eyeing Zak up.

His tongue separated her lips and dug deep, exploring, making her melt against him, moan at the back of her throat. Her fingers clutched his leather vest, hanging on for dear life. Because, damn it, a simple kiss from him made her weak in the knees. She should be pounding on his chest and insisting he let her go.

Not that he would, like the first night he snagged her and threw her over his shoulder to haul her up to his bed. She had pounded on him then, too. It hadn't done a damn bit of good.

The man wanted what he wanted. And what he wanted was her.

She was so screwed.

Almost from afar, she heard the catcalls and whistles, which caused Zak to bend over her, lean his weight into her, take her deeper, kiss her harder with a hand at the back of her head, pressing her close, keeping her connected.

When he finally released her mouth, she gasped for breath, because it felt like he'd sucked all the air from her lungs. And *somehow* her panties had gotten soaked.

Goddamn Zak.

"Might have to cut outta this party early," he murmured against her lips. There was no mistaking the kiss affected him as much as it had her. His eyes were hooded, his breathing as ragged as hers, and his erection pressed to her hip.

She quivered at the thought of him throwing her over his shoulder again and taking her back to his room to use some of those "wraps."

He grabbed her hand and took her farther away from the fire. But instead of heading inside and up the stairs, he pulled her over to a picnic table under an open pavilion and sat on the top of the table with his feet on the bench, encouraging her to settle beside him. Which she did.

Because she was a fool.

"Was gettin' too hot."

He wasn't the only one.

He wrapped an arm around her shoulders and squeezed, and, fool that she was, she moved to snuggle closer to him.

These last few days have involved a plethora of bad decisions. What was one more, right?

He didn't say anything for a few minutes. Not that she expected him to be chatty. He certainly wasn't that. But this life he immersed himself in fascinated her. Once again, because she was a fool, she didn't know how to keep her curiosity to herself.

She thought of the parking lot out back and how packed it had been. With cars, not bikes. "I thought this was a motorcycle club. Where are all the motorcycles?"

He paused a beat, then two. Finally, he asked, "Why were you hangin' by the bonfire?"

"Because it's cold."

"Babe. Just answered your own question." He snagged the beer bottle next to him and upended it, draining the last of the beer out of it. He slapped the bottle back on the table. She expected him to release a loud belch after downing the beer, but surprisingly he didn't. Maybe the man had some manners after all.

"There're some brothers who are diehards, have steel nuts, or are just plain nuts, who ride all year long. As soon as it warms up, you'll be on the back of mine. Don't worry."

"I wasn't asking because I was worried. There's no reason for me to ever ride on the back of a motorcycle."

Zak stared at her and simply said, "Babe," in the way that he did when he thought her comment was amusing.

But then his gaze flipped up and forward as something caught his attention.

A woman headed their direction, dragging a man behind her. Well, there was a switch. A woman taking charge of her man in this archaic club.

"Fuckin' Ivy," Zak murmured, shaking his head.

"What?"

"Bringin' a man here who don't belong. Pierce ain't gonna be happy."

"Who's Pierce?"

"Prez."

"Prez. President? Of the club?"

"Yeah. He ain't gonna be the only one not happy. Jag's gonna shit a brick."

She wanted to ask who Jag was, but the woman was getting too close. From what Sophie could see in the limited light and the glow of the bonfire, the woman had red hair, though not bright red, more like a deep auburn red. And she might be about their age. Maybe a little younger. No doubt she was really pretty. Really with a capital R.

"She's probably doin' it just to piss 'im off… *Hey*, Ivy."

As soon as this Ivy woman hit the concrete pad under the pavilion, she dropped her companion's hand like it was a hot coal. Most likely because she only had eyes for Zak. Though she gave Sophie a quick once-over before pinning her full attention back on the man sitting on the picnic table.

Well, then.

She didn't know who this Jag was, but this Ivy certainly held some interest in Zak. Yes, it was that obvious. She wondered if this Jag knew that little tidbit.

Sophie sat straighter and checked out the guy Ivy had dragged along. Normal guy, wearing normal clothes, normal haircut. Just normal. Probably had a normal job and normal boring life.

Sophie wondered if he was a fellow kidnapping victim. She gave him a smile, and he smiled back, but his eyes went quickly back to Ivy. Damn. Puppy dog eyes. He was crushing on her big time.

He definitely wasn't there against his will. Nope. Only Sophie was.

"Damn, Z, it's been so freaking long. Get your ass up and give me a hug."

Oh, she wanted to cop a feel of Zak? Not cool.

Zak hopped up, landed on his booted feet and enveloped the other woman in his arms. When she laid a kiss on his lips, Sophie shifted and frowned. And it wasn't a quick, friendly peck, either.

"Damn, you look good, Z. So glad you're home. We need to hook up."

Hook up? Like for coffee? Or for boot knocking?

Hold on...

"Yeah, we do."

Sophie's eyes slid to Zak, and she frowned harder at him. But his back was to her. Well, until he turned and introduced her. "Ivy, this is Sophie. Sophie, Ivy."

Ivy gave her a little smile and a small wave. Sophie said, "Hi," then tipped her chin in greeting... just like a biker chick would do.

She groaned silently and tried not to smack the heel of her palm into her forehead.

She was so fucked. She just needed to admit it and accept it.

Ivy brushed fingers through Zak's hair, sort of ruffling it, sort of caressing it. Heavy on the caressing. "I like it long."

"Yeah," was his response.

Yeah?

And when Ivy brushed her fingers over his beard, that's when Sophie felt her hackles go up. That was *her* beard. It belonged between *her* thighs.

And... *fuck.*

Shit.

Fuck.

The possessive caveman mentality was rubbing off on her. Zak was not her man.

Hell to the no.

"Well... This is Adam," she said, haphazardly flinging a hand in her date's direction.

"Where'd you find 'im?" Zak asked, acting as if the man couldn't hear him.

Rude.

Ivy lifted a shoulder, peeking over her shoulder at Adam, then looking at Zak again. "He wandered into the pawn shop one day looking for a TV and found me instead."

Zak gave a slight nod, his eyes flicking to Adam over Ivy's shoulder then back to her face. "Lucky him." He lifted a brow at Ivy. "You ask Pierce?"

And as if the two of them understood each other without using complete sentences, Ivy said, "All good."

"Right."

"Serious."

"Okay. Jag's here."

"I know."

"Just a warnin'."

"None needed."

Sophie watched the two of them talking like a tennis match. She tried to fill in the blanks but gave up.

"We'll get a drink soon and catch up," she finally said.

"Okay."

"Come work at the pawn shop."

"Ace don't need any more help."

"He loves you like a son, you know."

"Ivy, he don't need any more help," Zak repeated firmly.

Ivy lifted one shoulder. "Okay, Z." She leaned over, kissed him on the lips—the lips! *Again!*—slid a hand slowly down his chest, then spun on her heel, grabbed Adam's hand and dragged him back across the yard through the dark toward the fire, the kegs, and the coolers.

And the fool followed her like the lost puppy that he was.

Not that she had any right to be calling any other sap a fool. She was the queen fool right now.

Yes, she was.

When Zak hitched himself back onto the picnic table, she said, "She's got a thing for you."

"Nah."

"Yeah, *Zeeee*. A woman knows these things."

He stared the direction Ivy went then his head spun back to Sophie. "Nah. She don't want me."

"She called you Z."

"Everyone calls me Z. Don't mean shit."

Sophie sighed. "Fine. I imagined it."

A smile crept across his face and he leaned closer until he was practically nose to nose with her. "Jealous?"

"No."

"Think you are. A man knows these things." He pressed his lips to hers lightly, then pulled back. "She's Jag's, anyway."

"Huh. Unless Adam's nickname is Jag, I don't think so."

"Nah. She's Jag's."

"Did anyone let her in on that?"

"Jag did."

"Ah. So, I see it went over well. He got the girl."

"He'll get her."

Sophie shook her head in disbelief. "Damn you cocky-assed men. You all are something else."

"We see what we want, we get it."

"That simple."

"Yeah."

"Good to know."

"You already knew."

She sighed. She needed to extract herself from the conversation that was going to go nowhere but on a trip to frustration-land. "I need to hit a bathroom."

"Breakin' the seal?"

"What does that mean?" Already she needed to break out her Biker Translator app. Jeez. Whoever invented one would be a millionaire.

Zak just shook his head and flung a thumb towards the side door of the clubhouse. "Inside. Make a left. Be careful. Hurry back."

Be careful? Really?

"Who should I be careful of? The men or the women?"

"Both."

Sweet. Just what she needed to hear.

As she strode with a purpose through the yard, through a few pockets of people, Bikers, bitches, ol' ladies, *whoever*, she kept her eyes pinned to her destination. The side door of the clubhouse. No point in making eye contact with people she wasn't sure who would be friendly or not, nor did she turn around to glance back at Zak. Though, the second part was the hardest.

She stopped at the gray steel door and forced herself to not pound her head against it until she knocked some sense back into herself.

She stepped back quickly when the door swung open and a thin, lanky young male, wearing what was now a familiar vest, froze in place. He eyeballed her up and down. Then his inspection came to a stop on her breasts. See? The sweater made her breasts look *way* bigger.

"You new?" he asked her tits and licked his lips.

Sophie opened her mouth but nothing came out.

"You taken?"

What? He had to be at least ten years younger than her. Yikes. She opened her mouth wider to answer him, but before she could, he continued.

"You wanna go upstairs?"

Finally, a squeak escaped her at the balls on the kid. Her mind flashed back to being upstairs with Zak. She knew first-hand what went on upstairs.

A deep voice from behind her made her jump. "No, she don't wanna go upstairs with your weasel ass. Get gone."

"She ain't wearin' anyone's cut, Hawk," he protested, *finally* lifting his eyes. Though they stopped way above her. She had a suspicion there may be a giant standing behind her. But she was afraid to look.

"Don't matter, she's taken."

"By who?" he asked. The kid certainly had a set of balls on him to challenge the man behind her.

"Weasel, get gone or I'll rip that fuckin' cut right off you. Got me?"

Weasel? Weasels should never challenge a bird of prey.

"Hawk..."

"Keep it up an' the only vest you'll be wearin' is a sweater vest. An' it won't be in this clubhouse, either."

"She's just pussy. Bros before hos, brother."

A growl came from behind her. "Don't get banned, Weasel. An' you ain't my brother."

"Whatever, dude."

This so-called Weasel pushed past her, knocking his shoulder into hers causing her to lose her balance. Rude! Large hands caught her and turned her.

She looked up at one large "dude."

"Hawk," he practically grunted.

Huh?

"I'm Hawk," he repeated more like a human.

"Sophie."

"Know who you are. Not sure what Z was thinkin' by lettin' you wander 'round unescorted, 'specially since you ain't wearin' his cut."

She wanted to inform this Hawk that she never would be wearing any man's cut, whatever that was, but she thought it was smarter to keep that to herself for the moment. Apparently, if you weren't claimed, you were fair game. And this Hawk would have no problem throwing her over his shoulder and taking her upstairs. He probably wouldn't even be out of breath after doing so.

He looked a lot bigger and stronger than Zak.

"The baker."

She glanced up at him in surprise. "Yes."

"Your cake was the shit."

"Is that good?"

"Yeah. You bring another one?"

"No, sorry. The invitation to this... *shindig* was last minute."

"Next time."

Oh, here we go again. Once again, she thought it smarter not to tell him there wouldn't be a next time. Especially since every time she thought that, she was the one who ended up being wrong.

"Where you headed?"

"Bathroom."

He grunted and nodded toward the open door. "Inside on the left."

"Thanks."

"Hurry up an' then get back to your man."

Sophie's mouth dropped open. She snapped it shut, *once again*, deciding it was better to keep her opinion of his comment to herself. It would do her no good to get into verbal judo with the man, especially one she swore was four times her size.

"I'll do that," is what came out of her mouth instead. Weak.

He nodded in approval, gently pushed her inside, then shut the door behind her. Sophie closed her eyes for a moment, took some calming breaths in through her nose, out through her mouth, then headed left toward the bathroom.

The same music that was playing outside could be heard on the inside of what looked like the common room for the club, the room where she had first spotted Zak only three days ago. They must have the whole place wired with speakers. Luckily, she liked rock-and-roll, so the Black Sabbath song playing didn't bother her. In fact, she started singing under her breath as she spotted two doors. One said "chicks," the other said "dicks." At least the women's bathroom didn't say pussy, she supposed. She pushed the door open and—

A very large man with a very white ass was fucking a woman against the wall in the women's room. He wore a black leather vest with all the patches like Zak's and his pants hung down around his huge, heavy thighs. Since he was a lot bigger than the woman, she couldn't see who it was. She assumed it was a woman, but she couldn't be sure of that, either. Though the person taking the pounding's high-pitched wails sort of confirmed it. And there were some long, red painted nails digging into that very white, but muscular ass which was flexing powerfully as he pumped into whoever it was pinned to the wall in front of him.

He did have a really nice ass. Though it needed some sunshine.

"You joinin' us?"

The deep, amused voice startled her out of her frozen state. She looked up from his ass to his eyes. "No!" Sophie shouted, surprising herself, then stumbled backwards through the doorway, catching herself on the jamb before she fell, then mumbled, “Sorry,” and slammed the door shut.

Why was she apologizing? They were the ones that hadn’t locked the door. It was like they wanted to get caught.

The man’s chuckle was loud and deep enough she could hear it through the closed door which she now stared at, unable to get her feet to move.

“Diesel fucking someone in there?” came a female voice to her right.

So *that* was the man named after fuel.

“Yeah.” She glanced toward the woman, who was standing behind the bar, wearing a knowing smile. “He’s got an awesome ass,” Sophie whispered in awe.

“That he does.” The woman’s laughter sounded pretty and feminine, and she wore a welcoming expression. “I’m Bella,” she called out.

“Sophie.”

“I know. Hit the men’s bathroom, then come back out here. I’ll buy you a drink.”

Sophie nodded her head, then shot a glance at the door labeled “dicks.” “Nobody is fucking in there, right?”

“No. Only Diesel tends to fuck in the bathrooms. Says it takes too long to drag them upstairs.”

Oh.

“We’re used to it.”

Oh. All righty then.

Sophie pushed open the men’s restroom door cautiously, peeked inside to make sure the coast was clear, then she broke the seal.

Chapter Eight

Sophie sat at the bar, appreciating everything that was Bella. Who it turned out was Diesel's cousin. Real cousin. She was a beautiful woman, but there was something haunting behind her dark brown eyes.

Bella wore a loose black top with such a wide neck that it fell off one of her shoulders, which clearly had a large, colorful tattoo over the shoulder cap. Sophie wondered if it was more than the flowers she could see and where it ended. But she didn't feel brave enough to ask. The part she was most curious about was the statement on the front of her top in large white letters reading "Property of No One."

Now there was an independent woman, not putting up with any of the caveman bullshit which was clearly the norm around the club.

The Tequila Sunrise that Bella mixed for her was the bomb and Sophie couldn't put it down. Though she tried to savor it by taking small sips.

"You have to stay behind there all night?" Sophie asked her.

She wiped the bar down with a small towel, making slow circles like it was habit. "No. Just prefer it that way."

"Why not go out and enjoy the fun?"

Bella rose a single brow and stopped wiping. "Not interested in the so-called fun."

"Then why be here at all?" It wasn't like anyone had to pay for drinks, the private bar was a free-for-all to any of the members and their so-called "bitches." And even women who weren't their bitches. Or their ol' ladies.

Bella lifted her bare, tattooed shoulder. "I don't mind helping out. I'm used to it. It's family."

"Diesel being your cousin and all?"

"All the patched members are my brothers. But Hawk is my blood cousin, too. Dex is my real brother. Ivy my sister. Did you meet her yet?"

Did she ever.

"Yes... She have a thing for Zak?" Sophie asked before she could stop herself. She winced and Bella laughed.

"Yeah. Why? What'd she do?"

"Nothing. Just curious."

"Sure you are. Let me tell you something. Ivy's had a crush on Zak since we were all kids. It isn't anything. It won't ever be anything. Don't worry."

"Not worried. No reason to care."

"Right," Bella answered, throwing the towel somewhere under the bar.

"She's dragging some guy named Adam around," Sophie mentioned.

"Flavor of the month."

Interesting. "Zak said she's Jag's."

"He would."

Even more interesting. "Is that true?"

"Did you see Jag dragging Ivy around?"

"Nope." Not that she knew what Jag looked like.

"Then for now, it's not true."

"For now," Sophie repeated.

Bella shrugged. "Ivy does what Ivy wants. Despite what she needs."

"She need Jag?"

"She needs something. Not sure if it's Jag."

Sophie couldn't wait to meet this Jag.

"Speak of the devil," the other woman murmured.

Sophie followed Bella's gaze to where a couple was coming through the side door. It was a brother, obvious by his patched vest, and what appeared to be a stripper hanging all over him. She was weaving and so was he. But they weren't synchronized, so their hips kept bouncing off one another's as they wandered through the large room.

"That Jag?"

"Yep," Bella said, her eyes dark.

"Who's that with him?"

"Flavor of the minute."

Ah.

Sophie watched in fascination as Jag dropped onto one of the worn couches that lined the perimeter walls, dragging the heavily made-up woman on top of him. She immediately straddled his lap and started to sway with the music, which was now *Brown Sugar* by the Rolling Stones. Not quite lap dance music, but she seemed to make it work. And Jag didn't seem to mind if her rhythm didn't quite match the song. Suddenly the woman's skimpy top did a disappearing act, and her denim mini-skirt became pushed up around her waist as she continued to grind against the man's lap.

No one else in the room batted an eye at the woman's overly large, very obviously fake, bare breasts swinging in Jag's face.

"Is that normal?" she asked Bella, having a hard time ripping her gaze away.

"Yep. When Dawg brings his crew."

Her head spun to the woman behind the bar. Again noting there was something behind her eyes that made her older than her years. "Crew?"

"His girls."

Sophie shook her head.

"Heaven's Angels," she said, like Sophie should know what that meant. "Dawg manages the club's strip joint."

"The club owns a strip joint," Sophie repeated slowly.

"Yep. One of many of our businesses."

Businesses. Plural. So not just The Iron Horse Roadhouse.

"How did you become a part of the club? I figured you'd have to have balls hanging between your legs."

Bella laughed. "Damn. I like you. You might be perfect for Z."

Sophie ignored the last part. But she liked Bella, too, so far. She wasn't a skank like she had originally thought all the women would be hanging out at the party. She wasn't one of Dawg's strippers, either. And her shirt made it clear she was no one's ol' lady.

"My grandfather, Doc, is one of the two founding members. Which is why my uncle Ace, Dex, and my cousins are all a part of the club. It's engrained in our blood. Ivy's, too. We were raised here."

"He here tonight?"

"Doc? No. He's doing life at Greene."

"What's Greene?"

"A max security prison."

"Oh." Sophie spun her ass around on the bar stool, finally able to ignore the show behind her. She wanted to hear more about this Doc from Bella and it might take a while. "What's he in for?"

"Murder."

Sophie's jaw dropped open, then she snapped it shut. "Wow."

"Shocked?"

"I don't know."

"There's a lot of skeletons in the club's closet."

"I'm getting that."

"Nah. You haven't been around long enough to *get* it."

Sophie couldn't argue that point so decided to change the subject. "What other businesses do the club run besides the strip club and The Iron Horse out front?"

"Quite a few actually." She tilted her head toward a guy sitting down at the other end of the bar. "Crow runs In the Shadows Ink, a tattoo shop." Her eyes slid over to Diesel, who was now sitting with this Crow, his recent restroom conquest nowhere in sight. Though she couldn't get a good look at Crow since Diesel's massive body blocked her view. "D is the club's enforcer, plus runs all the security and protection, like the bouncers, for example. Takes care of any of the heavy hitting if you get my meaning."

Sophie's gaze landed on the good-looking, but huge man Bella had indicated. The one with the stupendous ass. And hip movement, if she had to admit it.

"Ace, my uncle, runs the pawn shop. Pierce, our club prez, runs the gun shop and range. We've got a body shop and towing company, too."

"Quite an enterprise."

"Yeah, we all work hard. And because we do, we all live good, too. It works." Bella slid another drink in front of Sophie, taking her now empty glass away.

When had she finished the first one? They went down so smoothly and Bella's information was fascinating so she must have been distracted.

Bella continued, "From the outside it may not seem like a good life, but from the inside... inside it is. Nothing like it."

Sophie sipped carefully at her second Tequila Sunrise. She wasn't a big drinker. Because of that, she was considered a lightweight, so she knew her limits. And she didn't think it was smart to get drunk tonight. From what she saw outside, and even inside, there were too many others doing that. She needed to keep her senses if things got out of control.

However, Bella had some skills as a mixologist. "You make great drinks."

"You make great cake."

"Thanks."

Bella tilted her head and studied her. "Maybe you can teach me to bake."

Sophie's brows rose before she could stop them. "You want to learn?"

"Yeah. I want to be good at something other than slinging drinks."

"Mixing the perfect cocktail takes skill, too." Sophie lifted her glass. "Especially drinks like this."

"Not at The Iron Horse. No one's asking for fancy martinis. A beer. A shot. Things are kept simple. I don't get to practice my skill too often. But I'm a pro at keeping the head low on a draft."

Whatever that meant.

"So, how'd you hook up with Z?"

Sophie took another sip, then shook her head. "I didn't."

"Right. He's only been home three days and from what I heard, he's been with you all three."

Damn. Word got around this place.

Bella laughed at her expression. "Yeah, nothing is sacred around here. Especially when you're getting it on upstairs."

"Wasn't my choice. It was a case of mistaken identity."

"Right."

"No, it's true. I certainly don't need a biker in my life. No matter what you say about the life."

"I hear you," Bella replied, then looked over Sophie's shoulder and shook her head, a smile curling the corner of her mouth. "It's not a life for just anyone."

"Too late. You got one," came from behind her.

She spun around to face Zak. "Well, I don't want one."

"Okay," he answered, shrugging. His gaze bouncing from her to Bella and back.

She hesitated. That was too easy. It was a trick.

He was tricking her.

"You took too long," Zak muttered.

"We were talking," Bella answered before Sophie could.

"See that." His head spun toward where Jag was now fucking the woman on his lap. The stripper still wore her mini-skirt high on her hips, but it was obvious that their grinding had become more than a lap dance. Jag's head was thrown back against the couch and the woman was giving a show to anyone who watched. Grabbing her tits, pinching her own nipples, crying out as if on cue.

Fake.

But still, they had an audience. Didn't seem that Jag minded, or Sophie would have guessed they would have moved it upstairs.

"Fuckin' Jag," Zak muttered, his eyes turning back to Bella. "Sorry."

"He's just trying to get under Ivy's skin," Bella said, not seeming to take offense that Zak's cousin was trying to get Bella's sister jealous. "He's just going about it the wrong way," she added.

"Damn straight."

Just when Sophie was about to point out that Ivy wouldn't know about it anyway, the woman in question walked in, Adam still in tow. Immediately, Ivy's gaze landed on the couch and Jag. And somehow, Jag's eyes just seemed to open at the right time and direct his gaze to Ivy, then shoot her a wide smile.

Ivy's whole body jerked as if she'd been slapped. After a second, she rolled to her tiptoes to say something into Adam's ear that made *him* smile, and then tugged him across the room and out the back door to the private parking lot.

And the whole time Jag's gaze followed them with a sudden frown, ignoring the stripper riding his pole.

Seemed to Sophie that Jag wouldn't ever own Ivy. Ivy already owned Jag.

"Fuckin' Ivy," Zak muttered, then shook his head. Zak's gaze landed on Sophie, then he said, "Finish your drink."

"Why?"

"'Cause you left me outside too long without you. Now, we need to go make up for that lost time."

Oh.

Bella's eyes found hers and the other woman pinned her lips together, trying to control her amusement. "See why I wear this shirt?"

"Don't give her any ideas, Izzy," Zak warned.

Izzy?

Bella frowned at the name, but ignored him. "You need help at the bakery? Like I said, I'd love to learn some baking techniques."

"I can't afford to pay you," Sophie said, regrettably.

"Understood. I wouldn't ask it. I'll be glad just to have a good teacher."

"Any time you want to stop by while I'm baking, do so. It's usually very early in the morning."

"I work The Iron Horse at night, so maybe I could come in early, then sleep in the afternoon before my shift."

Sophie nodded and smiled. "I'd like that." It was true, she really would. Not to mention, an extra pair of hands would be awesome. She couldn't afford to pay even a baker's helper right now. "I'm open Tuesday through Saturday."

"Babe," Zak murmured, suddenly nuzzling her ear.

Her hand automatically went up to cup his face. "What?" When she saw Bella's gaze looking at them with a knowing smile, she dropped it.

"We need to fuckin' go upstairs."

"Why?"

"Need to get what Jag's gettin', but just not in front of everyone."

Oh. Her pussy clenched at the thought of giving Zak a naked lap dance.

"So, finish your drink."

"I don't need to finish it."

"You anxious to go upstairs, then?"

She looked from him to the half full drink sitting in front of her. She could finish the drink and get a little more loose, lose a little more of her inhibitions before he had his way with her. Or... she could skip the rest and then he'd think she couldn't resist him.

She could never win with him. She decided to go with the drink, raising it to down the remainder in a couple swallows. Once it was empty, she slapped the glass on the bar top and blew out a breath to bolster herself.

"Ready?" he asked, his lips twitching.

"Do I have a choice?"

"No."

"Then, yes, I'm ready."

The crinkling of his eyes joined his twitching lips. "Good."

"Good," she repeated with a single nod of her head. She looked at Bella and announced, "I'm going to go get laid."

Bella pressed her lips together for a moment, as she removed the empty glass, before saying, "That you are. Have fun."

. . .

As Zak escorted Sophie across the common area, they couldn't help but pass close to Jag, who was now tucking his dick back into his pants. At the same time, the stripper was balancing on her platform shoes, tugging down her skirt.

"Classy," Sophie shot at him and gave Jag an exaggerated wink.

Jag's answer was a frown which made Zak chuckle and give his cousin a helpless shrug.

"You ever do that kind of shit?" Sophie asked, slowly following behind him.

Zak tightened his grip on her hand. "No."

"Well, that's good."

"No reason to."

"But if you had a reason to, you would?"

Zak winced when her tone of voice rose to a high pitch. "Said no reason to." As they reached the foot of the stairs, he turned to her. "Need me to carry you? Seems like it don't take much booze to get you wrecked."

"I'm a lightweight. I hardly ever drink."

"Apparently."

"But I'm not drunk."

"Good. Don't want you to be."

"And it's all about what you want, right?"

Zak frowned. His amusement with her was quickly dissipating. "If you say so."

"So."

Fucking hell.

"Babe," he warned.

"Babe," she echoed in a falsely deep voice.

"Someone needs a spankin'."

Sophie's eyes widened as she gasped, then lowered a second later, color rising into her cheeks. "Who needs a spanking?" she asked in a breathless whisper.

His amusement quickly returned. "Fuckin' lookin' at her."

"Me?"

"Yeah, you, babe. Now, you need me to carry you up? Or can you make it on your own?"

"I want to go home."

"Can take you home, babe, but you ain't gettin' out of my hand on your ass."

Her mouth parted and her breathing shallowed. She blinked at him. "I... uh..."

"Here or home?"

Her throat contracted as she swallowed. Hard.

He couldn't wait to sink his teeth into her neck as he was coming inside her. "Don't make me ask you again."

When she pursed her lips together, it took everything he had not to toss her over his shoulder and run up the steps. He was already as hard as a rock from watching Jag busting a nut in Goldie on the couch, so his patience was wearing thin as he waited for her answer.

"But I don't want to be spanked," she whined softly, eyes wide again.

Damn, she may not want it, but she was getting it. He'd make sure she liked it. Begged for it.

"Then walk upstairs with me on your own two feet," he finally said, stepping back and lifting an arm towards the stairs. "Go."

When she started trudging upstairs, he watched her ass rocking back and forth as she did so, though she bitched at him under her breath with each step.

He smiled. That ass would definitely feel his hand tonight.

Chapter Nine

ZAK CLOSED the door to his room, slid the lock home, then leaned back against the door.

"This room looks familiar," she said as she turned around to face him, hands on her hips.

His woman had a bit of an attitude. He needed to adjust it for her and knew exactly how to do that.

"It'll last longer this time. Promise."

"I'm relieved," she said, a little bit of sarcasm in her voice. Nothing he couldn't let roll off him.

"Thought you would be."

Her eyes dropped to the hard line of his cock in his jeans. "Did watching those two screwing on the couch do it for you?"

"Got me goin', I'll admit it. You?"

She only hesitated for a second before answering, "Maybe."

"You wet?"

"Maybe." No hesitation that time.

He smiled. Goddamn he loved her spunk. "Strip for me."

She raised her brows. "There's plenty of other women around here who are good at that."

He shook his head. "Don't want other women. Want you, babe. Strip for me."

"Why, Zak? Why do you want me?"

"You do it for me."

"How do I do it for you?"

She did it for him in so many ways. The reasons didn't all have to do with her looks or curves, though that's what caught his attention first. Her resistance to his *charms* was another. He didn't want an easy, boring lay. He liked the chase. He wanted a feisty attitude, which she had in spades. Her owning her own business was a plus, too. Showed she had drive, smarts. And she wasn't looking for a man to take care of her. She could do it on her own.

Though, now that would be unnecessary because he wanted to take care of her. Protect her. Crazy that this instinct of his had kicked in almost immediately. More like as soon as he realized he'd been mistaken on who she was a couple nights ago while she was in his bed.

He dropped his hand to his hard-on and rubbed it with his palm over his jeans. "They may have gotten me started, but it's now all you, Sophie. This is all you."

As she watched him slide his hand up and down his length, she licked her lips. Damn if he didn't feel that all the way down to his balls.

"Strip for me, babe. Show me your moves."

She whispered, "I don't have any moves."

"Oh yeah you do. Show me," he encouraged just as softly, letting his gaze run over her from top to toe. The woman had curves that wouldn't quit. Her breasts, her lips, her hips, and those thighs which would be wrapped around him shortly.

And her boots... Her wearing heeled knee-high boots was the cherry on top of the sundae. Or more like the icing on top of the cake.

Her eyes narrowed. "You going to spank me if I don't strip for you?"

"Yeah."

"Then I'm not stripping."

Swallowing became difficult, his mouth suddenly arid like a desert. She wanted him to spank her.

Holy fuck.

She had just whined downstairs that she didn't want that. What happened between there and here?

Maybe the alcohol was hitting her right about now.

"You want me to spank you?"

"Didn't say that."

"You don't want me to spank you?"

"Didn't say that, either."

"Babe," he said, his voice cracking. "C'mere."

"No. You *c'mere*," she repeated him.

Within a flash, he was dragging her sweater over her head, ripping her jeans down her thighs, dropping to his knees to unzip her boots, sliding them off, caressing her legs, her feet, as he slipped her jeans and panties down the rest of the way. He nipped her inner thigh, and she yelped, then giggled.

Giggled.

She wanted this as much as he did. Or she was now totally tanked. He hoped it was not the latter.

Fuck! She was a pain in his ass.

Why she couldn't admit it and felt the need to fight it... Zak pushed that out of his head. Didn't matter, he was getting it, she was getting it, and he was going to make sure it was good for both of them.

Like last night.

And the night before. When his life had reset and restarted. His luck had definitely changed the minute he spotted Sophie here, in his world.

As he perched on his knees at her feet, he looked up her body and she was staring back at him, her hair falling around her face, her eyes dark, heavy. She reached behind her as he watched, unclasped her bra and let it fall off her arms to the floor next to them.

Her scent permeated his nostrils. Hot, wet, wanting. He bit back a groan. When she cupped both of her breasts and squeezed them together, brushing her thumbs over her hard nipples, he couldn't fight his reaction any longer.

"You like that?" she asked.

She was teasing him. Driving him mad, driving him to the edge. "Yes, babe. Show me more."

She rolled both nipples between her thumbs and forefingers, twisting and pulling. Her mouth dropped open and so did his when he released a ragged breath.

"Fuck, Sophie, *fuck*. I'll never get tired of watchin' you touch yourself."

She released one nipple, dragging her hand over her sternum, down her belly. Over the small stripe of dark hair until she cupped her mound, slipping one finger between her folds.

He sat back on his heels to watch her. This was so much better than her stripping. So much better.

His cock pressed painfully against the zipper of his jeans. He needed to rid himself of his own clothes, but he was afraid to move. Afraid to break this spell of hers. If she stopped what she was doing, he might shatter.

"Show me how wet you are, babe. Let me see."

With two fingers, she separated herself and he focused on her pink, slick pussy. Wet for *him*. Wanting *him*.

But he needed to hear it from her lips. "That for me, babe?"

"Yes... No one but you."

Her words caused his heart to squeeze, his cock to twitch. Fuck! He needed to get naked right now.

"I want your mouth on me, your beard scraping my thighs."

"Now or after your spankin'?"

She hesitated, her eyes getting darker every second she considered what she wanted.

He couldn't wait for her to answer. He pushed to his feet, dropped his cut from his shoulders, tossing it on the nearby chair, then unbuckled and yanked off his boots, throwing them to the side with a thump.

Zak's eyes caught movement. Sophie was backing toward the bed, her eyes pinned to his. "Stay where you are." She froze and tilted her head in question.

He ripped the Henley over his head and flung it wide, then peeled his jeans and boxers off his legs. When he straightened, he was pleased to see she listened, which made him even harder.

He moved past her to sit on the edge of the bed. "Babe," he held out a hand. "On my lap."

She came over, her tits peeking from between her long mane of hair and he couldn't wait to suck one of those peaked nipples into his mouth. As she began to straddle him like Goldie did Jag, he stopped her.

"No, babe. Not like that. Lay across my lap."

She hesitated, meeting his eyes for a moment, before settling over his lap, offering her sweet, sweet ass.

"You sore?"

She nodded, her face in the mattress. "A little."

His cock jerked at not only from having her draped over him, but the memory of sinking deep into her virgin ass last night. Unfortunately, that would not be repeated tonight. Fortunately, he had a large supply of wraps in his room to sink into her warm, slick pussy instead.

He trailed his fingers down the crease of her spine, marveling at her perfect, ivory skin. Her ass wouldn't be pale for long.

Skimming his fingers along her ass cheeks, he tapped each one lightly, then bent over and kissed them. One, then the other.

He smacked each one again, a little harder this time. She didn't move. Not a shift, a flinch, nothing.

He swept his hands over the curves of her cheeks and down her thighs to the back of her knees and back up.

He smacked each cheek again, making sure it stung a little. This time she jerked on his lap, which didn't help his situation of being ready to blow, but she remained quiet.

"Bein' inside you last night, babe... Fuckin' loved how tight, how hot you were 'round me. But watchin' your ass become pink right now... Damn. Tonight might be a toss-up with last night whether this is my best night yet since my release."

When his hand came down again, he cracked her right cheek hard, causing her to yelp and jerk against him.

"Like that?"

"Yes… Harder."

Holy fuck. His girl liked to be spanked. How lucky could he be? "Sure?"

"Yes! Harder!"

He smiled at her enthusiasm before putting a little weight behind the smack to her left cheek. She cried out again, but this time didn't move.

"Again," she said, her voice muffled in the fleece blanket covering the bed.

"Damn," he whispered, watching her ivory skin turn pink and red.

He moved back to the right, giving it his all, making sure this one stung, too. A lot.

She squealed and her hips shot up.

But as they dropped back down, he decided he couldn't take anymore. Not one more second. He needed to be buried deep inside her. But what she said next stopped him cold.

"Smack me there."

There.

"Where?" he breathed, wanting to make sure he understood what she asked.

"There," she moaned, opening her thighs. "Not so hard, though. Just enough to make me feel it."

"You're fuckin' killin' me, babe."

"Do it, Zak. Smack me there."

He tapped her labia lightly with his fingers, avoiding his palm, being careful. When she groaned into the blanket and ground her hips against his lap, he did it again. Harder.

She released a curse.

"More?"

"Yes. Yes. Do it again."

"Sophie."

"Do it!"

His brows shot up his forehead and when he did it again, she squirmed in his lap. Precum beaded at the tip of his cock and his balls tightened.

Fuck.

He had no idea two nights ago when he grabbed his little baker and carried her upstairs that it would lead to this. Lead to something he would never get enough of.

Which was her.

He would never get enough of her.

"Again," she begged.

No. No. He couldn't take anymore. He drew a finger between her folds. She was soaked.

As much as he wanted to taste her arousal on his tongue once again, he knew he was at his limit. Her rosy ass cheeks, her flushed, swollen pussy lips. He just couldn't...

He hooked her under her arms and, with a twist, threw her onto her back. He came up on hands and knees over the top of her, his arms and legs caging her in. Her mouth was parted, her lower lip swollen as if she'd been biting it.

He dipped his head and stroked it with the tip of his tongue, then pulled away long enough to rip the nightstand drawer open, pulling out a wrap.

He tore it open with his teeth and rolled it on quickly, his cock twitching in his own hand.

"Bend your knees an' spread 'em, babe."

As soon as she did, he settled between her sweet, luscious thighs. With one thrust, he took her fully, filling her. His eyelids dropped low at how hot and tight she felt as she squeezed around him, her body trying to pull him deeper.

Fuck. Fuck. Fuck. He needed to hold himself together. He needed to make this last. Not like two nights ago.

He wanted to savor this feeling for a while. To enjoy their connection.

But when she moaned his name, he lost his mind, pumping furiously into her. Her calves wrapped around him, her heels dug into his ass, her arms lassoed his neck, pulling him closer.

"Zak, fuck me," she breathed. "Fuck... me."

His nostrils flared, and he swallowed hard. Her eyes were closed, but he needed to see her. He needed her to see him.

Him.

He wanted to make sure she knew it was him deep inside her. Not anyone else.

"Sophie," he struggled to get out.

Her eyes fluttered open.

"You see me, babe?"

"Yes," she whispered.

"Who am I?"

She hesitated and he watched as confusion clouded her face. "What?"

"Who's deep inside you? Makin' you feel this way?"

Her eyebrows furrowed. "You."

"Yeah, me. Who am I?"

"Zak... You're Zak."

"Yes, babe. I'm Zak."

"I know."

He tilted his hips, taking longer, slower strokes, grinding against her each time he hit the end of her. "Just wanted you to realize who's inside you."

"Just shut up and fuck me."

Zak's hips jerked, and he chuckled. "You got it, babe."

He shifted until he had her knees pinned to her chest with his. Then he slammed her until her hips bucked wildly underneath him.

The harder he fucked her, the louder she got. He wouldn't be surprised if they heard her wailing all the way downstairs and over the music, too. But he wasn't going to stop her. No way.

Best. Sound. Ever.

He curled his body over her until he could shove his face into her neck, inhaled her scent as she squeezed and pulsed around him.

"That's it, babe," he murmured against her neck. "Give it to me. Give me everything. Fuck, gonna lose it soon."

He sank his teeth into her neck and she arched it back, crying out. "Zak, I'm coming."

Sweetest sentence he ever heard in his life. And it was coming from his babe's mouth. "That's it... squeeze me tight," Zak said against her ear. "Christ, you're so fuckin' wet."

When the ripples started around him, clenching and releasing his cock, his balls squeezed and he let go inside her with a grunt.

After a moment, he dropped lower, still trying to keep his weight off her. But he didn't want to, he wanted to cover her, wrap her around him tighter, feel her damp skin against his.

He pressed his forehead to hers, trying to steady his breath.

"Baby," she said with a satisfied sigh, her eyes closed.

He stilled and sucked in a breath. "Babe, look at me." She opened her eyes, meeting his. "You just call me baby?"

"No."

"Yeah, you did."

"You imagined it."

"No way."

"Yes."

He tipped his chin. "Babe."

"Yes, baby?" she teased softly.

He smiled, then slid out of her to fall to her side, gathering her close. "Yeah," he breathed, satisfied with her response.

A MOMENT LATER, he rolled away from her with a groan. "Let me get rid of this. Don't move."

He didn't have to worry about that, there was no chance of her moving. He'd pounded all the bones right out of her body. Sophie's eyes tracked the way his muscles moved under his heavily tattooed skin as he walked to the tiny bathroom attached to the room. She wondered how many of the other rooms had a private bathroom like this.

Then, she wondered whose ass was nicer, his or Diesel's? She let out a little snort at her pervy thought. She rolled onto her side, facing the direction he went, and propped her head on her hand while she waited.

When he came back out sans condom, she couldn't pull her eyes from his lean, cut body. The man did not let himself go while in prison, no, he didn't. She opened her arms when he got closer and he climbed onto the bed right into them, pulling her tight against him.

A little sex and she'd totally lost her damn mind. Never in her life did she think she'd be cuddling with some tattooed, ex-con, badass biker. Even if he was a sexy one. In fact, her friends and family back home would probably want to commit her if they knew.

But they'd never know. She'd make sure of it. She'd enjoy a few hookups with him, then get back to concentrating on building her business, making it a success. He'd probably get bored soon anyway, move on to his next conquest. There were plenty to choose from downstairs, and she was sure there were more who would jump at the chance at being a part of a club of all alpha men.

While she appreciated an alpha male, she wasn't so sure she wanted to be stuck dealing with one on a daily basis. They were too bossy, too controlling, too possessive. Too everything.

Though, she had to admit, some of his bossiness turned her on. Some. Not all. Some frustrated her, too.

She tended to be the domineering one in her past relationships. Which usually didn't bode well for said relationships. So, she could appreciate a man who would stand up to her, give it back to her as good as she gave it. She didn't have any respect for a man who acted like a whipped dog, but still—

"Babe."

"Hmm?"

"You're squeezin' the shit out of my arm. Everythin' okay?"

She tried to focus on his face which was just inches away. She softened her grip on his bicep, slid her hand down his arm, and as soon as she got close to his, he intertwined their fingers together. He lifted their clasped hands to his lips, kissing each of her fingers. That's when she realized he was missing something most of his "brothers" wore.

Jewelry. Lots of silver. Turquoise. Brass. Chunky rings on almost every finger. Earrings in one or both ears. Medallions and pendants hanging on chains and cords. He had nothing adorning him except his tattoos.

Which was perfectly fine with her. She was never into men who wore jewelry, even badass stuff. Not that she ever had a bona fide badass before.

The man studying her with the beautiful blue eyes was her very first.

"No rings. No necklace. Nothing. Why don't you wear them?"

"Used to. Had to take them off when I went inside. Just haven't pulled them back outta storage. Most my shit's at Ace's farm. Haven't had a chance to get out there. Only got out a couple days ago, remember?"

How could I forget?

"But you normally wear that type of stuff?"

He shrugged. "Yeah. Why?"

"Nothing."

"Ain't nothin', babe. You don't like it?"

It was her turn to shrug.

"Don't matter to me, either way, Soph. You don't like it, won't wear it."

"Really?" He'd change one of his biker ways for her? No.

"Just one ring that's important to me, anyhow."

"Please don't tell me it's a wedding ring and you're married." *Jesus.* That never even crossed her mind.

He laughed and dragged a finger along the hair falling across her face, tucking it behind her ear. "No. Got no ol' lady. Well, I'm wrong. Now I do."

"If you're talking about me, I'll have you know, I'm not an old lady. I'm only thirty-three."

He feigned shock. "You're thirty-three?"

"Yeah."

"Damn, you're old." She shoved him and he chuckled. "You're older than me."

She stilled and her eyes shot to his. "What?"

"Yeah. Got me beat by a year."

Her breath returned. "Oh. A year isn't much."

"Cougar."

"What?" She laughed. "No."

"Yeah. That'll be your biker bitch name," he teased. "Cougar." He did a bad impression of a growling cougar.

Sophie rolled her eyes. "Biker bitch. Never."

"Yeah. My ol' lady." He pointed a finger at her. "You." Then he pointed the finger at his own bare chest. "Mine."

Grunt. Grunt. Chest Pound.

"You don't own me."

"The day you wear my cut, I do."

"I have no idea what a cut is."

"My colors."

She shrugged, still confused.

"The leather thingy with the patches I wear over my shirts."

"That grungy vest is called a cut?"

"Not grungy."

"Yeah, okay."

"It's not," he insisted.

Sophie snorted. "Stinks, too."

"You sayin' I stink?"

"That dead cowhide with those dirty, grimy pieces of cloth stuck to it does, yes."

Zak tangled his legs with hers, quickly flipping her over onto her back. He rolled his weight over her to pin her to the bed. He stared down at her. "So, you want me to wear it every time I'm fuckin' you. That what you're sayin'?"

"Every time? You think there's going to be a next time?" Her voice lifted at the end until almost a squeak.

"Sure of it. This is the third. There'll be a fourth. Maybe in a few minutes."

"Huh."

"What?"

"So freaking cocky."

"Yep."

"Okay, so why is this one ring important to you?"

"It was my granddad's."

"One of the bikers who started this club."

"Yeah. How'd you know that?"

"Bella."

"Bella's breakin' you in." He sounded way too satisfied with that fact.

"I doubt that's why she told me. I was curious about the club."

"You can ask me anything. Just don't always expect an answer. Won't tell you club business."

"Why not?"

"Babe," he simply said as if that should answer it all.

"Because I'm a woman?"

"The way it is."

"I can't understand why the women all put up with it."

Zak lifted his shoulders. "We give good dick."

Sophie's breath stuck in her throat for a moment. Then it rushed out of her when she laughed. "What?"

"Yeah."

She shook her head, a tear popping out with how stupidly funny that statement was. "You all give good dick, so that's why they stick around and deal with your archaic ways?"

"Yeah."

"Holy shit," she murmured. "Seriously. That's hilarious."

"But true."

"Sure it is. You want me to test it out?"

"Fuck no. You don't touch any other brother down there. An' they know better than to touch you."

"Is that so?"

His jaw got tight and his eyes hard. "Yes, Sophie, that's so. You don't fuck around with another brother's woman. Not if you wanna live."

"Loyalty's important then."

He didn't answer, instead he dropped back to her side and threw an arm over his head, staring at the ceiling. "We do things differently. Our own rules. Our own justice."

"Apparently."

"Don't fuck with another brother, Sophie. I'm tellin' you now. Won't be good for you. Won't be good for the brother."

His voice sounded hard, serious. And she realized just how serious since he was using her actual name instead of his normal easy-going "babe."

He turned his head and pegged her with his gaze. "Got me?"

She sighed. "Believe me, there's no chance I'm sleeping with anyone downstairs. I shouldn't even be sleeping with you."

His eyes softened a little. "We haven't slept yet."

She whacked his arm. "You know what I mean."

"Yeah, babe, I do."

Back to "babe." Her relief at that disturbed her.

"Bella tell you my dad an' brother are cops?"

Sophie pushed up onto her elbow and stared into his face. His eyes flicked to her then back to the ceiling.

"Really?"

"Yeah," he answered on a sigh.

Well, that was a twist she didn't expect. And he didn't seem too happy about it. But then, she was sure the feeling was mutual. She wondered what it would be like to be on one side of the law while your son was on the other. Had to be tough, maybe eat at you.

"Well, that's... Tell me how you became a biker then. What made you choose this way of life?"

"Family."

"What do you mean? You just said your family aren't bikers. They're cops, which are far from bikers. Different end of the spectrum."

"Not that far. My granddad, Bear, was a Vietnam vet. Came out of the fuckin' war in the early seventies an' started this club with a soldier buddy named Doc, Ace's dad. So, it's in my blood. It's in my father's blood. My brother's, too."

"But they resisted."

"Not entirely. They belong to an MC, too."

She shook her head. "How can that be?"

"They both belong to the Blue Avengers. A cops' MC."

"Cops have a biker club?" She was having a hard time wrapping her brain around that new piece of information.

"Yeah. Not uncommon."

"I never knew that."

"Have to remember, babe, cops are part of a brotherhood. An MC is a brotherhood. Goes hand in hand."

"Guess they're not *out*law bikers, but *in*-law bikers." She snorted. Though Zak didn't laugh. Whatever. *She* thought it was funny and clever.

"Mitch, my dad, wanted to keep free of the outlaw life. Especially after his pop got killed. My uncle Rocky embraced it. Also wanted revenge. But now he's doing life inside because of it. So is Doc."

"That's not a way to live."

"No, it's not. That's why my generation of brothers, which includes my cousins, have worked hard to pull us outta that life. Make it legit. Can't afford to lose any more of us to the concrete box above ground or the one below. Just gotta keep Pierce on board."

"Pierce," she echoed.

"Prez."

"I remember. Why wouldn't he be on board?"

"Prefers the old ways."

"Murder and mayhem?"

"Somethin' like that. Eye for an eye. Retribution. Revenge. Reckonings."

"They never did anything about you being set up yet, though, right?"

"Didn't say that."

"So, they did?"

"Didn't say that."

"If they didn't, will they?"

"Club business, babe. Not for your ears."

"Yes, because I'm a silly woman."

"Didn't say that, either."

Sophie blew out a noisy breath and flopped to her back, deciding the ceiling must be interesting to stare at, since he was staring at it so hard.

As she studied the stained drop ceiling over the bed, a thought rushed her. One of the local cops stopped in the shop on a regular basis ever since she opened its doors.

"What's your brother's name?"

"Axel." His eyes narrowed. "Why?"

Oh.

No.

"Nothing. Such a unique name. You said he's a cop, right?"

Gah. She was stumbling over her words. And Zak didn't miss anything.

"Babe, just had that fuckin' conversation."

"I know. I'm just trying to wrap my head around it."

She didn't want to tell him that his cop brother was a regular at the shop. Didn't want to? Hell, she wasn't *going* to.

"And how's your relationship?"

"Non-existent."

Not. Good.

She had a suspicion that Axel stopped in because he was interested. But she wasn't telling Zak that. It could be he was just being friendly. He certainly was nice to look at. She rolled to her side, studying Zak's face. Why hadn't she noticed the similarity?

Maybe because Axel's hair was cut super short and more military-like, while Zak's was on the longer side. And the beard... Had to be the beard, too. But the blue eyes. Yes, she could see the resemblance.

He always came in for her red velvet cupcakes with the cream cheese icing. He'd only buy one because he said he needed to stay in shape. And even under that uniform with his Kevlar vest and his duty belt, she could see he was fit. And hot. Couldn't forget that part.

Plus, she got the joy of watching him eat it. Lick the icing from the top in a way that made her squirm.

Fuck.

She had actually hoped he'd ask her out on a date. Especially after she noticed he didn't wear a wedding ring. In fact, she made sure to keep red velvet cupcakes in the display case every day.

That was Zak's brother.

Shit. Guess that date was out of the question now.

Because that would be just weird.

Wouldn't it?

Crap.

She should have been more forward with him. Asked *him* out for a date. Because maybe if she *had* been dating Axel, *this* may not have happened.

Though, Zak hadn't asked any questions before hauling her ass upstairs two nights ago. If she had been dating Axel, it might have put a bigger rift in their relationship after his brother fucked the woman he was dating. It might have been a little worse than a rift. It might have turned into a war.

And she would have been the cause of it.

Apparently, the brothers had similar tastes.

"What are you thinkin' about?"

Shit. Uh... "Round two."

A smile spread over Zak's face, his eyes darkened, and his expression looked hungry. He rolled over her, pinning her wrists above her head. "Can do, babe. Top or bottom?"

Chapter Ten

SOPHIE CAREFULLY EXTRACTED herself from Zak's sleeping embrace. Surprisingly, the badass biker liked to spoon. Every time she had shifted throughout the night, he shifted with her. Not one minute had gone by where he wasn't touching her in some way. Could be he was worried she'd slip away during the night.

She padded to the bathroom to take care of relieving her bladder, then quickly returned to his bed. She glanced at her cell phone sitting on the nightstand. 3:30 AM. At least the loud music finally died down. She imagined the clubhouse common area was littered with bodies sleeping or passed out and was sure the rooms upstairs were full, too. She couldn't miss the hooting and hollering, the moans, groans, and curses through the thin walls throughout the night. Which meant others had heard her and Zak, too.

Her cheeks bloomed with heat at the thought. Though she had no reason to be embarrassed, at least they hadn't had sex on the bar or a pool table in front of everyone. Now *that* would be embarrassing.

Mumbling, Zak's hand came out from under the sheet to curl around her naked hip. She looked over her shoulder at him. He still seemed to be sleeping since his eyes were closed and his lips slightly parted as he breathed steadily. She should leave. She really should.

But to be honest, she liked falling asleep in his arms after their third round of getting down and dirty last night.

Down and dirty. Zak told her that *Down and Dirty 'til Dead* was the club's motto, that the founders had come up with it way back when the club was established in 1974. A long time ago. This club had deep roots in this town. Although, she couldn't understand the appeal of the lifestyle, the club was, in a sense, its own community. Had its own laws to live by. Any issues amongst the members, they handled it internally. Club business never leaked outside their membership. If it did, it was serious and would be handled as such.

She was more fascinated by the club, its members, its way of life than she wanted to admit. Though Zak said they lived "easy and free," she didn't think they did. They answered to each other. They were tied down to businesses. She had a feeling their sense of "freedom" only came when they were on their motorcycles hitting the open road.

And right now, the weather in Pennsylvania was too cold for that.

Sophie turned on the small lamp on the nightstand. It had a bandana over the ratty lampshade to give the room a soft red glow. Though, not bright enough to wake up the man sleeping next to her.

She shifted until she laid close enough to study his naked chest. She'd never been with anyone with more than one small tattoo. And even that was years ago. Zak had more tattoos than naked skin.

She wondered how many he got while in prison. She couldn't imagine being locked up for a whole decade for something you didn't do. That had to be frustrating as hell. It made her a little sad, too, since he was now thirty-two and went in when he was twenty-two. He missed a lot of his young adulthood. Instead of exploring life, living hard and free, he'd been pacing a cell. Most likely forced to watch his back every minute of every day.

How heartbreaking to have to live like that.

Her eyes roamed his chest and his tattoos. Each one seemed to tell some sort of story. She brushed her fingers over the Lady Justice designed as a sexy pin-up girl holding the scales of "injustice" over his right pectoral muscle. The scales were unevenly tipped to one side. A permanent reminder of what happened to him with his conviction.

Her fingers trailed over to his left pec where a black and gray portrait of a man's face sat over his heart with the letters "RIP" underneath it and "BEAR" over top. Zak's grandfather, murdered by a biker from another outlaw club.

His right bicep sported a Harley emblem clutched within a Bald Eagle's claws. In full color, it was impressive and very well detailed.

A waving American flag dressed his left bicep with the words "Live to Ride" over the top and "Ride to Live" under the flag.

The words "Down & Dirty 'til Dead" ran down the inside of one arm in large black lettering. She traced each block letter with her finger. Then there were numerous smaller tattoos filling in the negative space, including a black and gray skull with a red bandana wrapped around its forehead, a smoking cigarette clutched between its teeth. The letters DAMC were inscribed on the bandana.

She pushed the sheet lower on his hips to see the beautiful, but huge, red and black Scarlet Viper that literally snaked around his hips.

The sheet started to rise. Either someone was awake or enjoying her light touch in his sleep very much.

She slipped the sheet farther down, watching him grow before her eyes. Without looking at him, she slid down the bed, circled the root of his cock with her fingers, and took him into her mouth.

His breathing no longer sounded steady, his fingers no longer relaxed as they dug into her hair, guiding her mouth up and down his length. He tasted salty and all male. Cupping his sac with her free hand, she squeezed gently as she came down on him, taking as much of his length as she could. His hips rose off the bed in an attempt to go even deeper.

Without releasing him, she moved in between his open legs. She wanted to watch him, see his reaction. When she tipped her eyes to his, he met hers and didn't let go as her mouth glided up and down his steely length over and over. His face went from lax to tense in moments. His body tightened, stilled, and he grunted loudly.

"Babe," he groaned. His fingers gripped her hair so tightly that the pull on her scalp started to burn. But she didn't care. Like the spanking, it turned her on. She wanted him to pull harder. "Fuck."

She traced the tip of her tongue along the thick vein, then around the crown and back down, sucking the delicate area where his cock met his balls.

"Fuckin' Sophie," he groaned again. "Need to stop."

No, she wasn't stopping. If sucking him made her wet, watching the pleasure on his face made her even more so. Her pussy clenched with need, making her think she might even climax at the same time he did without anything or anybody even touching her.

She lifted her head only long enough to say, "Wrap," and then her mouth, her tongue, continued its path, made his hips twitch, his fingers tug. One hand released her hair, and she heard a clatter as he desperately reached for a condom.

She paused again. "Hurry."

"Fuck," he barked.

When she heard the tear of the wrapper, she moved faster up and down, sucking harder, taking him deeper down her throat.

"Fuck! Now, Soph, now."

She released him and crawled over him as he rolled the condom on. And no sooner that he had it unrolled, she straddled his hips and sank down, taking him fully. Within seconds, her head fell back, a cry escaped her lips, and she came, rippling around him.

Zak grunted as she continued to ride him hard, not even pausing during her orgasm.

"Babe, look at me."

She opened her eyes and met his blue ones, darker than she'd ever seen before.

"Goddamn," he muttered, digging his fingers into her hips. "Come again."

"Touch me."

One hand moved from the curve of her hip to her breast, cupping, squeezing, teasing the hard nub of her nipple. The other dropped lower, finding her sensitive clit, circling, pressing, flicking... then squeezing until she almost shot up off him. When she slammed back down, the waves of her second orgasm took her under. He went with her this time, grunting louder, cursing.

Then he stilled.

She stilled, too, weak and boneless once again. Her pussy still throbbed while his cock continued to pulsate deep inside her.

"Swear to Christ, you're going to be the fuckin' death of me," he groaned.

"Then we won't do this again."

"Rather die that sweet death than go without."

"Just remember, this isn't a thing," she said softly, more to remind herself than him.

"Babe, was a thing the moment I laid eyes on you."

She was afraid he was right.

THIS *THING* WAS GETTING out of hand. Slowly, this biker club was embedding itself into her life. No, not just embedded, painfully implanted. She hadn't signed on for this. Not at all. Just sleeping with one of the members apparently caused a snowball effect that was getting out of control.

When she came down to the bakery this morning—early, like really early to get a start on Tuesday's menu items—she was surprised to find someone else in the shop and it wasn't Bella, who was due to show up for her first day of training.

The person who hunched over a new hole in the wall was certainly not as pretty as Bella, nor as verbal.

He was of the grunt, grunt, chest pound variety. And a large one at that.

Though, she couldn't help but check out Diesel's ass now that it was covered in denim. Sophie tilted her head trying to decide if his glutes looked better in jeans or naked.

It was a toss-up.

When her gaze rose, she realized that the huge hulk of a man was glancing over his shoulder at her, wearing a smirk.

Damn. Busted.

"Could've joined us."

"I already got a lecture about doing other 'brothers.' So, no thanks, I don't need that hassle."

Not that she would ever consider doing a threesome with this hulk of a man, with not only another woman, but in a bathroom to boot.

He grunted and went back to doing whatever he was doing. Which, by the way, she had *no idea* what he *was* doing.

"Is there any reason why you broke into my shop so early in the morning?"

"Got shit to do."

Sophie pursed her lips, wondering if it was worth the frustration to keep asking questions. She decided it wasn't and moved closer, attempting to peek around him, which was not an easy feat since he was not only tall—too tall to see over his shoulder—but wide with what looked like solid muscle. She could only imagine the rest of him matched his glorious ass.

But, again, he wasn't worth the headache, and she already had a bad one that wouldn't go away. Even if that headache was good in bed.

How he put that hole in the wall without her hearing it upstairs, she'll never know. He probably punched the hole with his beefy hands.

"Security system?"

Grunt.

"Right. Well, I assume you want coffee. I'll get a pot going."

Grunt.

Sophie bit her lip. "Did you at least unlock the front door for the customers?"

Grunt.

She smothered her laugh. Surprisingly, she wasn't frustrated. It was turning out to be quite entertaining to bother him with questions.

"Did I tell you your ass is really fine?"

No grunt this time. His eyes slid to her and he gave her a chin lift. She was starting to really understand this caveman speak.

"You're welcome. If I had to see someone's naked ass, I'm glad it was yours. Absolutely spectacular."

Diesel returned his attention to the wiring he was working on, but not before Sophie noticed his nostrils flare.

"I mean, Zak's is really nice. But yours... damn," she finished off in a whisper, then wandered to the front of the shop, unlocked the front door, but schooled the amusement off her face before turning and heading back behind the counter to start the coffee.

"Bella comin'?"

Sophie froze with a full scoop of coffee grounds in her hand. She quickly dumped it into the coffee filter before it clattered to the counter and made a mess. "Yep."

"You teachin' her to bake?"

"Yep."

Without looking at her, he nodded his approval, then went back to twisting wires.

She grabbed a fresh apron, threw it over her head and tied it around her waist. Running her fingers over the embroidered stitching across her chest, *Sophie's Sweet Treats,* she felt some satisfaction that this place was all hers. And the bank's, of course.

And apparently, her shop would be a little safer after today. Though she couldn't figure out from what.

The bells above the door jingled and she glanced up to see Axel pushing through the door, his eyes landing on Diesel. He frowned, then his eyes cut to her, which made Sophie frown. Diesel also frowned at Axel's appearance.

Appeared no one was happy at the moment.

Shit.

She was sure Diesel would report Axel's visit back to Zak.

"Guess you don't trust the PD to protect you?" Not a hello, or how ya doing, nothing. Right away Axel was on the defensive, which made Sophie's frown deepen.

His defensiveness probably had to do with the mountain of a man he couldn't miss.

"I do."

"Then why is Diesel putting a security system in your shop?"

And, of course, they knew each other.

"I don't know; he won't answer me."

Axel cocked a brow. "You didn't hire him?"

Now she really saw the resemblance to his brother. "No."

"Diesel won't answer you because Diesel don't answer to a woman," Diesel grumbled.

"Well, there you go," Sophie said, throwing up her hands and giving Axel a large, mocking smile.

"Diesel," Axel warned in a low voice.

"Fuck off, Axel," Diesel shot back his own warning in a much louder voice.

How about that? They knew each other by their first names. Even better.

Axel's eyes went hard. Diesel's went harder.

Sophie stepped between them, breaking their stand-off. "Got new flood lights out back, too. I didn't ask for them, but I got them anyway."

They had been installed yesterday, though no one had broken in to do it. Some guy named Squirrel, who wore a DAMC vest claiming he was a "prospect," had installed them. At least he actually had been somewhat polite.

"Really," Axel murmured.

"Yes, with motion sensors. I don't know who's going to pay for them, either."

"Not for you to worry about," Diesel muttered, his back now to them as he finished wiring the security panel.

"Well, again... there you go. I just have to keep my mouth shut, I guess."

Diesel screwed the panel closed then turned, hands on his hips, shoulders tense under his worn, just as grimy as Zak's, leather vest. "What're you doin' here, Axel? This is DAMC territory."

Axel, who in contrast wore a neatly pressed police uniform with a whole lot of weapons hanging around his hips, snorted. "No, it's not."

Diesel raised his brows and waved an arm around the bakery, then toward Sophie. "*This* is DAMC territory."

Axel looked pointedly at Sophie and frowned. "Say it ain't so."

"It ain't so," Sophie echoed. She was certainly not DAMC *territory* as much as Zak thought otherwise.

"Bullshit," Diesel grumbled.

Axel turned his back to the larger man to confront her. "You hooking up with him?"

Sophie felt the blood drain from her face. "No!"

"I ain't so bad, lady. Jeez," Diesel muttered.

She sighed. "That's not what I meant."

"No, he's bad, Sophie. Stay away from him," Axel said.

"Listen, *cop*, an' I'm bein' nice here. You chose your path, so go walk it. The club's got everything covered here."

"You want me to go?" Axel asked her.

"I, uh... Ah, *fuck*," she ended in a pained whisper, slapping a hand to her forehead as the bells jangled again.

It couldn't be Bella coming through the door. Nope. Of course it had to be Zak, his eyes hard, his jaw hard, as his gaze landed on Axel. Well, this morning was starting out perfectly!

First thing out of his mouth was, "What you doin' here? This is club territory."

"I already heard that song and dance, brother."

"You're not my brother." Zak shot a thumb toward Diesel. "He's my brother."

Axel's lips thinned to an angry slash. "Since when did Sophie's bakery become DAMC?"

"Since the moment I stepped outta that concrete box you threw me into."

"I didn't throw you in there."

"Same shit."

Axel shook his head. "No, Zak. That's what happens when you step in shit. It clings. It's hard to scrape off. The smell lingers. And don't be dragging Sophie into your shit. She doesn't deserve it. She's a decent woman trying to make a decent living. Don't drag her down."

Zak's eyes narrowed on his brother. "Yeah, guess we ain't decent enough for decent women."

Axel shrugged. "I see the women you have hanging around church, Z. Don't think I don't. Sophie isn't that. She isn't a house mouse, she isn't a sweet butt, she isn't ol' lady material. You know it. I know it. Leave her alone."

House mouse? Sweet butt? She had no idea what those were. But now was not the time to ask.

Zak's head jerked back and his gaze bounced from his brother to Sophie and back to his brother. He took a step forward and Axel tensed. "What's it to you?"

"Nothing. She landed in town trying to start a business, plant some roots. Don't poison it."

Zak shook his head, his eyes hot with anger. "No, Axel," he said with deliberate slowness. "What's she to *you*?"

"Coffee anyone?" she asked, her voice loud, but not loud enough, apparently, to catch their attention. "Coffee, Diesel? Zak? Axel?"

Zak's eyes landed on her. "Babe."

"Babe?" Axel echoed, his brows now pinned to his hairline. His gaze shot to Sophie. "How'd you get tangled up in this shit?"

"I made a cake," she whispered.

Shit.

"You made a cake," he repeated slowly.

"Yeah, Ax, she made my homecomin' cake. You know, I'd just got outta the joint an' my family here," he jabbed a finger at Diesel, "was kind enough to pick me the fuck up."

Axel at least had the decency to look somewhat embarrassed, but his expression turned to stone quickly once again. "Didn't know you were getting out."

"Right," Zak scoffed.

But Sophie didn't miss the pain that crossed Zak's face. It was there and gone in a flash.

"So, I'll ask again, *brother*. What is *she* to *you*?"

Axel smiled and Sophie's stomach flipped when he said, "I like to eat her *cupcakes*."

Ah, shit.

Zak stiffened, then scrubbed both hands over his face and his chest heaved before dropping his hands. His eyes landed on Sophie who froze in place at their intensity. "That right?"

Her mouth dropped open. Then she whispered, "Red velvet."

Maybe that wasn't the best answer because Zak acted like she had just said something else entirely. Like red velvet was code for her—

In a flash, Zak was nose to nose with Axel, his hands fisted, his chest puffed out. Before Sophie could react, Diesel suddenly became the reasonable one.

Surprise!

"Don't!" Diesel's sharp bark made her jump. "Don't, brother, you know punchin' a pig is an automatic agg assault." He stepped closer to the real brothers, who had eyes locked on each other.

"If I punch him, it'll be 'cause he's blood, not 'cause he's a cop."

Damn, they were siblings, they should be hugging since they hadn't seen each other in so long. But no, here they stood in *her* bakery getting in a pissing match.

Over nothing. Fucking red velvet cupcakes.

"Don't matter, brother. You're DAMC, he's a pig. They'll take you down anyway they can get you."

"I'm not going to be taking Zak down. If he wants to try to swing at me, more power to him." Axel turned his face, just slightly toward Diesel, so he could have eyes on both. "And stop calling me a damn pig. We've known each other since we were in diapers."

"Don't mean you ain't a pig. Went to the dark side."

Axel's laughter was sharp. "I went to the dark side? No, I escaped the dark side. I'm the light."

At his own reminder of his life's choice, Axel stepped back. Sophie breathed a sigh of relief.

"Sophie doesn't need the hassle of the club."

"You don't know what she needs," Zak growled.

"So you think," Axel pushed.

Zak's jaw tightened again, but he finally uncurled his fists. He took a long breath and stepped back, too, giving the two of them some distance. At least, from what Sophie could tell, out of sucker punch range.

As the bells jingled again over the door, Sophie thought, *not a good time for a customer to show up.*

But it wasn't a customer, it was Bella, who appeared frozen in place barely inside the door, her eyes glued to Axel, her face pale.

Axel tensed once again when their eyes met. "Izzy," he said softly.

What was up with that? His demeanor totally changed and his calling her that got her moving.

"No, Ax, you know I'm not using that name anymore."

"That's who you are to me."

Her mouth got tight as she pushed past the three testosterone-filled, chest-pounding men to come behind the counter. "I'm not her anymore," she said, her eyes now on Sophie, but unreadable. "Why are you here?"

"He eats Sophie's cupcakes," Zak grumbled.

Bella gaped at Zak. "What?"

Sophie closed her eyes for a second, took a breath, then said, "He likes my cupcakes. Holy hell. Okay, Bella and I have work to do. Everybody out. There will be no cupcakes if we don't get started."

"Babe." Zak.

"But—" Axel.

"Ain't done." Diesel.

All at the same time.

"Out!" Sophie yelled. "All of you."

Zak smiled. Diesel grunted. Axel frowned.

"Babe, D ain't done."

"I don't care. He can finish up another time. Get out. All of you." She stepped from behind the counter and waved her hands at them as if she was shooing them away. "Out. Go. I can't take any more of this macho crap today."

Diesel looked to Zak, who gave him a slight nod. The larger man gathered his tools and left, the door slamming behind him.

Sophie pinned her eyes on Zak. "You, too."

"Not leavin' 'til he does." He tilted his head toward Axel, whose attention was still centered on Bella.

Hmm.

Interesting.

Just then, the portable radio on Axel's hip squawked, which jerked him out of his trance. He moved toward the door. Saved by the squawk.

"I'll stop back later for my cupcake. Extra icing, please."

Sophie sighed. He just *had* to say that in front of his brother.

With a last glance at Bella, he opened the door. Then he said, "Keep your ass clean, Z. I don't think Mom can take you doing another ten-year stretch."

"An' what about Dad?" Zak shouted as Axel closed the door.

Zak received bells jingling as his answer.

Sophie's heart squeezed for him. "Zak..."

Zak shook his head, came over and wrapped an arm around her hip, pulling her against him. He pressed a thumb under her chin and tilted her head up. "Thanks for helpin' Bella," he whispered before pressing his lips to hers.

His kiss was light, but it still sent a thrill through her. "Be back later for my *cupcake*, too."

Great.

She hated the fact that though his bossiness annoyed her, the thought of him coming to her later, or tonight, gave her butterflies.

Actual butterflies.

She needed a strait jacket and a reservation for a padded room.

"Your concern about my safety is really cute. But I'm a Philly girl. And compared to that, this is small town America. If I can survive the big city, I can certainly handle Shadow Valley. I'll be fine."

"Don't underestimate Shadow Valley, babe. There are more layers to this town than you might realize. Better to be safe than sorry."

Right.

He released her and swaggered out of the bakery.

And Sophie watched his hips the whole way.

She was doomed.

Chapter Eleven

ZAK ACCEPTED the draft beer from Bella as she worked her way down the bar. He took a sip before placing it in front of him.

The Iron Horse was quiet tonight. A few regulars. But for the most part, nobody was being rowdy and the music from the jukebox was louder than the patrons. Sometimes it could be the opposite.

The crack of the pool balls from the tables, along with the murmurs of the customers who were eating unhealthy bar food and drinking drafts or downing shots, were much more pleasant sounds than the shouts of inmates, buzzers, and the clang of a closing cell door.

After handing off beers to a couple guys down at the end of the bar, Bella stopped back in front of Zak and leaned a hip against the bar.

He loved this woman like a sister and was disappointed to see that her carefree attitude, and fun-loving, wild personality had been permanently changed.

"How'd it go today?" he asked.

She gave him a small smile. "Good." She studied him for a second then said, "She's awesome, Z."

Nothing he didn't already know. "Yeah," he agreed, trying not to smile like a fool into his beer.

"She knows her stuff, too. It was fun. I ended up covered in flour and powdered sugar but it's a small price to pay to learn what she does."

He was pleased they got along so well. "Lemme guess. You made red velvet cupcakes."

Bella—he was having difficulty thinking of her as anything but Izzy—let her gaze drift away. "Yeah. They're good."

"I'm sure they are. But I'm also sure that's not the only reason my asshole cop brother stops in there."

Bella still wouldn't meet his eyes.

He traced a finger down his sweating pint glass. "Somethin' going on, Izz?"

"Bella, Z. You know that."

"Bella, then."

"With what?"

He lifted his beer but hesitated with it held only an inch from his lips. "That whole shit with Axel."

Because if something was going on between Axel and Sophie, he needed to know. If anyone would tell him, Bella would.

"Nope."

Zak took a sip, then frowned and shrugged. "Okay."

She lifted a brow, a clear sign she couldn't believe he'd let it drop.

"You goin' back tomorrow morning?"

Her eyes lit up at his question. It was nice to see her excited about something. In the few days he'd been home, he hadn't seen enough of that from her. It pained him.

"Plan on it."

"You wanna give up tending bar?"

She sighed. "Not sure. Tips are half decent, but the clientele can be a challenge, as we all know."

"No shit. No need for bouncers tonight, though."

"There's one here."

Zak twisted his neck to look toward the front door. "Who?

"Lincoln."

That's when he noticed the prospect nicknamed "Abe" standing by the front door, arms casually crossed over his chest. The one Jayde couldn't keep her eyes off of. As long as they kept their hands off each other, Abe would last another week as a prospect.

Just then, two other prospects rushed through the front door and Abe went into full defense mode. Squirrel and Weasel shot the other recruit a quick glance but didn't stop to talk to him. They jogged up to Zak instead.

"Z!"

They were both out of breath, which made him frown. Something was up. The hair on the back of his neck stood at attention. "What?"

"Shit went down at the bakery. Pierce told us to get you right away," Squirrel said.

Zak pushed off the stool to his feet. "What shit?"

Weasel joined in. "Not sure. We just got a call from Pierce to let you know. Said he was tryin' to get a hold of you. Some kinda shit with the Warriors."

What felt like a bucket of ice water rushed down Zak's spine. Fucking Shadow Warriors, still pulling their shit. "Sophie okay?"

"Dunno."

"What the fuck you mean you dunno? What'd Pierce say?"

"He said get you. Tell you to get over there. You didn't answer your phone."

Zak pulled his phone out of his back pocket and saw he had a half dozen missed calls and texts from the club's president.

Fuck.

He must have accidentally put his phone on silent. He skimmed through the texts but they didn't have any good information.

He glanced at Bella. "I'm out. Anyone comes lookin' for me that's where I'll be. Call Diesel. Let 'im know if he don't already." He turned back to the prospects. "You two stay here with Abe. Watch the bar an' Bella. Got me?"

He got two "yeahs" as answers. He gave them a sharp nod, a pointed look, and pushed through the swinging double doors to the kitchen. Once he came out of the kitchen into the clubhouse side, he started hauling ass toward the door to the back parking lot where he'd left the piece of shit car parked. It had better start.

Luckily, it did. He pealed out of the lot, kicking up stones as he floored the accelerator.

When he arrived at the bakery, no spots remained out front. He pulled around back and parked next to Sophie's car. After jimmying the locked back door to the bakery, he rushed through the empty kitchen area into the shop, then stopped dead.

Mitch Jamison, in full uniform, had his arm around Sophie, and it looked as though he was consoling her.

That was *his* job. Not his father's.

Fuck.

Mitch's eyes rose to meet his, and he frowned. Not a welcoming *hey-son-glad-you're-out-of-the-slammer* smile. Nope. More like a *what-fucking-mess-have-you gotten-into-now* frown.

"She yours?" Mitch asked, surprised, and Axel looked up from whatever he was writing in a spiral notebook.

"Yeah," Zak answered but didn't move closer. From where he stood, he let his gaze wander over Sophie to make sure she appeared whole. No blood, but definitely tears. Her face was streaked with them.

Shit.

Mitch shook his head. "Not smart. The Warriors aren't done with you."

"They're not done with the club in general," Ace said coming through the wide-open front door of the bakery. "Zak ain't the only one they've targeted."

"Who else?"

"Club business," Zak cut in as if that said it all.

And apparently it did.

"Fucking club business," Axel muttered, turning his attention back to his report. He scribbled something and then slapped the notebook shut, tucked it in his back pocket, slid the pen into the front pocket of his uniform shirt then spread his feet wide, looking at Zak directly. "This is the shit that I was talking about earlier, Z. This right here. You claim this bakery... Hell, you claim Sophie as DAMC, and this is the type of shit that happens."

Zak kept his mouth shut. He wanted to push his father out of the way and take over comforting Sophie, but he also needed to know what happened. Instead of asking Mitch or Axel, he looked directly at her. "Tell me."

She swiped at her eyes. "I heard a crash downstairs, and I thought it might be you breaking in again, so I came down. Luckily I did, someone threw a... a..." She looked toward Axel.

"Molotov cocktail through her front picture window," he finished for her. "And she *is* lucky. But only because it didn't explode. Especially with her being so close."

Zak's gaze bounced from the broken window to the broken bottle on the floor with a greasy rag laying nearby. His heart stopped.

"Is this the same old beef, Ace? Or is there a new one?" Mitch asked the older man.

Ace pursed his lips and ran a hand down his long salt and pepper beard. "No beef."

Mitch sighed and shook his head in disbelief. "Right."

Sharp laughter came from Axel as he shook his head, too. "Really? No beef? We all know that's bullshit. There's been conflict forever. All the way back to when Bear got killed."

"How you know this is Warriors?" Zak asked Axel.

"Who else would it be?"

Zak shrugged, attempting to be a picture of innocence. "Dunno. Thugs from the Burgh?"

Axel's eyes cut to Sophie. "You have any known enemies, Sophie? Anyone have a vendetta against you? You step on any other baker's toes? Crush any cake dreams?"

Zak's hackles rose as the cop questioned his woman. He held out his hand to her. "Babe, c'mere."

Mitch's arm tightened around her shoulders. "You don't have to listen to him."

Jesus Christ, his family kept proving that they just weren't that. "Babe," he repeated slowly. "C'mere."

He was relieved when Sophie pulled away from his father and moved closer. But, unfortunately, not close enough.

"I thought you said that being with you would keep me safe. Now it looks like being with you is just the opposite."

Axel laughed. "He told you that being with him would keep you *safe*? Right. Is that a pickup line that works? 'Cause I'll have to try that one. Though, if I tell a woman that, it'll be true. I wear a badge, not a cut with a target on it."

"Goddamn it," boomed from the doorway. And everyone's heads swung that direction. Diesel and Hawk both shouldered their way into the bakery, doing a cursory inspection of the damaged window and toeing the broken bottle. "This is war."

"I did not just hear that, Diesel. Right?" Mitch said, hands on his hips above his duty belt.

"Knew I should've stayed an' finished the job," Diesel grumbled.

Mitch's eyes narrowed. "What job?"

"Diesel's installing a security system in the bakery," Axel explained. "They have it all under control," he finished, the sarcasm thick in his voice. "You know, since this is DAMC territory."

"Right," Mitch responded, eyes flicking to Zak, who ignored him and once again held a hand out to Sophie.

"Babe."

Sophie shook her head, her eyes still shiny with tears. "No, Zak. No. I want no part of this... *beef* or whatever. I don't want anything more to do with your club."

"Or you," Axel finished for her.

"She didn't say that," Zak said, shooting daggers at his brother.

"Or you," Sophie repeated softly.

Fuck.

Not good. One little Molotov cocktail and she was ready to toss him to the curb.

"This is my business. My life. This isn't a game for me."

"Babe, c'mere," he pleaded. He could step forward and grab her, taking her into his arms, but he preferred she'd make the choice to come to him. Plus, it would show the two cops standing in the middle of the bakery that she *chose* to be with him.

But apparently, he was wrong. She moved away, giving him her back instead.

Fuck.

Fuck.

Fuck.

He wasn't going to beg in front of his club brothers, or Mitch and Axel. He would deal with this after they all cleared out.

Right now, he needed to get her front window boarded up as well as clean up the spilled gasoline and the broken glass.

"You step up security everywhere?" he asked Diesel, feeling as if he was stepping back into the president's boots. Even though he wasn't. But security needed to be tightened right now at every DAMC business. At least until they knew whether this was a hit-and-run by the Warriors or they were in town to play hard.

"Already done," Diesel answered. "Gotta get the prospects out here with some plywood."

"I'll call 'em an' get 'em in motion," Ace said, stepping through the broken glass and heading out the front door.

"This shit's gotta stop," Hawk grumbled. "You guys done here yet?" he shot at Mitch and Axel.

Axel's lips thinned, and he turned toward Mitch. "We have enough?"

Mitch gave a sharp nod. "We know who did it. There's nothing concrete, but again, they don't want us serving justice anyhow, so we'll get no cooperation on either end."

"Nope. We'll take care of it," Diesel barked.

"Right," Mitch answered. "We'll up patrol in the area."

"Not necessary," Zak said.

"Not your choice," Mitch answered. "You going to be okay, honey?" he called out to Sophie, who was now behind the counter, hugging herself and staring blankly at the broken window. "They're going to board up your window. Right, Hawk?"

"Right."

Sophie didn't look at any of them, just nodded as if in a daze.

"We'll get you a report for your insurance," Mitch added. "Axel will stop by tomorrow to check in on you." He paused, then added, "And get his cupcake."

Zak's eyes narrowed as he looked at his father. "Think you're done here."

"Right," Mitch answered, looking his oldest son over. "I'm sure you do." He glanced at Sophie, "You need anything, you have our cards. Give us a call, Sophie."

"Okay," she said softly, still not looking at them.

Zak watched his blood walk out the front door and only then did he feel his muscles loosen a bit.

Hawk's eyes flicked from him to Sophie and back. "We got shit handled here if you wanna go get your shit handled."

Zak wrapped his fingers around the back of his neck and sighed. "Yeah."

"We can see ourselves out after. We'll get the fuel cleaned up, too."

"Thanks, brother." They clasped arms and bumped shoulders. "First thing tomorrow, yeah?" he said to Diesel, wanting to make sure the security system was finished as soon as possible.

"Yeah, sure thing, brother."

Zak nodded, then went behind the display counter to wrap an arm around Sophie's waist and guide her back through the kitchen. She felt wooden to his touch, but then, he couldn't blame her. Someone was out to not only destroy her business but maybe hurt her, too.

A muscle ticked in his jaw and his fingers tightened on her hip. "Let's go upstairs, babe."

She shook her head and stopped at the bottom of the stairway. "I'll be fine. I want to be by myself."

That was never going to happen, but he knew if he said that he might never get upstairs.

"Let me at least make sure you get into your apartment safely."

She hesitated for a moment, then sighed and started up the steps. Zak sucked in a relieved breath.

Once upstairs, he shut the apartment door behind him and twisted the deadbolt. She pulled away from him and turned. "You can go now."

"I'm either stayin' here with you tonight or you're comin' back to church with me."

"I have to get up early again in the morning. I'm not leaving. And I'm not going to have them chase me out of my home."

That settled it. "So I'm stayin' here."

"Aren't you the target?"

"But you're a part of me, babe."

At his words, her eyes went from unfocused to heated. "That's what *you* think and now that's what *they,* these *Warriors* or whoever, think. But no one asked me what *I* think." She stepped to the middle of the room, crossed her arms and spun to face him. "I know I keep asking myself this, but... how the hell did this happen?" Her shaky whisper made his gut twist. "How did I become a part of *you*? And how would they know this? I only met you five nights ago."

"News travels fast, Sophie. Especially when I made it pretty clear you belong to me."

"Why?"

Why? So many reasons why. But he knew she wouldn't want to hear any of them, wouldn't accept them, or would think they were stupid.

He only did what he'd known his whole life: once you've found a good woman, you claimed her as yours. A man was only as good as the woman at his back.

His parents might not be living the life, but as the stories go, his father had claimed his mother just the same. As far as he knew, they were still happy together. He hadn't heard anything to the contrary.

"I didn't think you'd have a good answer. Tell me, why do I want to be a part of something so freaking archaic? I mean, the little I've been around you all, I can see it. It's the brotherhood, then your bikes, then the 'bitches.' I assume I'm in that last category, or would be if I was your 'woman.'"

He shook his head. "It's not like that for everyone, babe. It's not."

"Seriously, what was this house mouse and sweet butt stuff Axel mentioned?" She lifted a palm before he could answer. "No. I can only imagine. I probably don't want to know."

"That ain't you."

"Maybe not. But they exist, right?"

She made a noise when he didn't answer. She moved toward her kitchen, leaned a hip against the counter and crossed her arms over her breasts, effectively closing herself off from him. "Be honest with me, Zak, why do these Warriors have a beef with you?"

He shouldn't tell her. He needed to keep club business just that, but she needed to know. She got caught up in this mess with the rival club which meant she deserved an answer. She wasn't a house mouse, she wasn't a sweet butt, she wasn't one of Dawg's strippers. She was to be his ol' lady. She would never agree to that if he wasn't completely honest with her.

When he went to step closer, she held up a hand.

"I can hear you from there. Speak."

He scrubbed a hand over his beard and sighed. "Began over territory. The Shadow Warriors were nomads with no home turf. Wanted to settle. Came through a sleepy town called Shadow Valley. Felt that the name fit 'em, I guess. Had no idea the Dirty Angels already established their mother club here. The club at the time was small, still growin'. But none of the originals were givin' up the territory that the club claimed. Push came to shove, Bear ended up dead. Went back an' forth for a while 'til my uncle Rocky helped Doc take out a bunch of 'em when they least expected it. They moved on but never forgot."

"They're the ones that set you up."

Wasn't a question, so he didn't confirm her suspicion. "They show up now an' again. Don't know if they're just ridin' through or comin' on purpose. Gotta feelin' this was on purpose."

"Them setting you up was on purpose, too."

He tucked a thumb in his jeans' pocket, dipped his head to stare at the toe of his boot, and gathered his thoughts. He wanted this woman so much that it tore at his insides to see her putting up a wall because of shit the club has had to deal with for almost thirty years. Almost as long as both of them have been alive. They were both caught up in something neither of them had a hand in.

Axel was right; she didn't deserve any of this. He was surrounded in shit. And she was so much better than shit. But he still needed to tell her the truth. He'd have to deal with whatever happens afterward.

SOPHIE STEELED herself as the words continued to cross his lips.

"When I was prez, rule was not to engage 'em. Be on the defensive, yeah. Be on the offensive, no. Don't need the bloodshed that happened back in the seventies an' eighties happenin' again. Dead brothers, dead family, others servin' life, might as well be dead. Got us nowhere fast. Things needed to change. I stepped up. Even though I was still wet behind the ears, they accepted me holdin' the gavel. Had good brothers by my side. Changed things. Worked on makin' 'em better. Strengthened the club, expanded, filled the coffers so we all could live good. Warriors want what they don't have. We wanna keep what we worked hard for."

"But I'm not part of the club." She meant this as a reminder to him. But, in all honestly, it was more of a reminder to herself.

"Babe, the moment I dragged you upstairs, you became a part of the club. I claimed you."

Dragged. Claimed. She felt like she'd fallen in some parallel universe. One she couldn't pull herself out of.

"Claimed me." She shook her head and laughed bitterly. "You guys act like there's nothing wrong with that. Nothing archaic about it." She pulled the imaginary knife out of her heart and threw it at him, hoping to cut him just as deep. "I'm sorry, but I can't be some man's property." This needed to end. So she went for the kill. "Especially a biker's."

A muscle ticked in his jaw. "Biker's not good enough," he muttered, running a hand through his hair, then hooking it around the back of his neck and squeezing.

"*You* chose this life. I," she pounded her palm against her chest, "didn't. I don't want to live this way. I *refuse* to live this way. To live in fear. To live in the shadow of a man who doesn't see women as equals. Don't make me give up my dream and go back home to Philly to get away from this shit *you* dragged me into."

His eyes got hard as he rumbled, "You're not goin' anywhere."

She didn't want to go anywhere, but she might have no choice. "If my bakery ends up destroyed, I'll have nothing left."

"You got me."

Her eyes bugged out, and she threw her hands up. "Great. Give up my lifelong dream for an ex-con biker. Sounds like solid planning for the future."

"I can take care of you."

She started to pace, but stopped dead and whirled on him. "Don't you get it? I don't want to be taken care of. I'm not a piece of property." She pointed at him. "You. Don't. Own. Me. I've known you for less than a week... *Fuck*! I've been forced to have sex with you."

He winced. "Weren't forced."

She talked over him, her arms swinging wildly. "I've been propositioned to sleep with a guy named *Weasel*!"

"What? I'm gonna kill that—"

She cut him off. "I was invited to a threesome in a bathroom. With another woman, by the way."

"What?" His eyes narrowed. "Who? Why didn't you tell me—"

She kept going, ignoring him. "My bakery was attacked. Not to mention, I was almost killed! Why would I want *any* of that?" She began to pace again. "What's next? Am I going to be kidnapped? Held for ransom?"

He held out a hand the next time she walked by him. "Babe." She swatted it away.

"*And* I have a name!" she practically shrieked. "It's Sophie, goddamn it!" She paced some more. "It's not like I love it but it's mine. This bakery is mine. And I'm my own person. I've survived the last thirty-three years without you taking care of me and will survive another thirty-three." She halted abruptly and turned, hands on her hips. "So let me use words you'll understand..." She pointed to the door. "*Get gone*!"

Zak closed his eyes and dropped his head. "Don't do this, Sophie," he said quietly to his boots.

"Don't make me call SVPD and have them physically remove you, Zak. Because I'm sure that Axel would love to do just that."

His head came up, the pain deep within his eyes. "Don't do this, Sophie," he repeated softly.

Sophie squeezed her eyes shut, steeling herself from the hurt in his, and inhaled deeply. Even with her eyes closed, she couldn't rid herself of seeing the tightness around his mouth, the defeat in the curve of his shoulders.

She opened them. He hadn't moved. "Go live your life, Zak. You're free now. Stay that way."

"Not a life without you."

Her heart squeezed painfully, and she did a slow blink, fighting back the sting. "You've only known me for five days."

"Knew you the minute I saw you," he whispered.

It killed her when he said things like that. He knew how to play with her heart, her emotions. "You thought I was a stripper," she said, reminding herself how they met.

"Wouldn't have mattered to me if you were."

Sophie groaned in frustration and turned away. "Get gone, Zak," she said quietly.

"At least let Diesel finish your security system."

She nodded but couldn't face him. "I'll find a way to pay him."

Silence met her and when she finally turned she realized he "got gone."

She should be relieved. But for some insane reason, she wasn't.

Chapter Twelve

Sophie pushed open the swinging door between the bakery's kitchen and the shop and froze.

At the front by the register, Bella and Axel were leaning toward each other over the display case, eyes intense, and whispering fiercely. Axel had a hand outstretched, cupping Bella's face.

Suddenly their harsh whispering stopped and both sets of eyes turned to her. Axel quickly dropped his hand and they straightened. Even from where she stood, Sophie could see the color in Bella's cheeks.

Interesting.

In the three weeks since Bella started helping out, Axel stopped by more often. Even on his days off he'd show up in his casual clothes, which he had never done before. Sophie had to admit that the man looked good in either a uniform or jeans and a worn T-shirt. And when the day was colder, he would wear a black leather jacket and look like he would fit right in with the DAMC. She could picture the two brothers sitting side by side on their Harleys.

Though, Sophie doubted it would ever happen.

However, Axel's excuse for his daily appearance was that he was now hopelessly addicted to her cupcakes. And it didn't matter if they were red velvet or not.

She unfroze herself and moved forward.

"You didn't make red velvet cupcakes," he teased her as she neared.

"No." She hadn't because she wanted to find out if he was addicted to something other than that excuse. Or more like someone. She wasn't sure if it was her presence bringing him in, since Zak had been thrown to the curb which she was sure Bella told him.

She had a thought after seeing what she just witnessed. Maybe now it was Bella's presence that drew him.

Hmm.

"You guys grew up together, right?"

Axel's gaze flicked to Bella then landed back on her. "Not really."

Bella stepped back from the counter and busied herself by assembling pastry boxes. "Ax wasn't allowed to hang out with us biker kids. We were a bad influence."

"But you knew each other," Sophie prodded.

"We went to school together and we're sort of related," Axel answered.

"Sort of?"

He continued, "The Doc-Bear connection. Not by blood, though," he added quickly.

"No, not by blood," Bella clarified a little too quickly as well. "Why?"

"Nothing. I was just wondering. I find this whole DAMC family tree interesting."

"Have things been quiet?" Axel asked Sophie. She knew what he was really asking: if Zak had made himself scarce.

He had, surprisingly.

Though, it kind of hurt that he gave up so easily.

What the hell was she thinking? She kicked his ass out of her place, out of her life for a good reason. She didn't want anything to do with any crazy biker beefs where people actually died. Not to mention, went to prison *for life.* All because they fought over some town. There were plenty of other towns in Pennsylvania she was sure weren't "claimed territory" by some other club.

She just had to stop thinking about bikers, beefs, and men with tattoos wearing grimy leather vests. Especially ones who gave her multiple orgasms. Or more like one biker in particular.

She ground the heel of her palm into her right eye.

Axel wrapped his fingers around her wrist and pulled her hand away, looking concerned. "You okay?"

"Yes, fine."

His lips flattened. He didn't believe her. "It's for the best, Sophie. Take my word for it."

She snorted. "Right, says the man who had no problem cutting his blood brother out of his life."

Axel frowned. "You don't understand. I'm a cop. I can't have anything to do with an outlaw biker club. Blood or not."

That's when Bella broke in, color high in her cheeks. "What the fuck, Axel? You know better than that. The club hasn't been a one percenter in a long time. Shit's different now. Has been. And if you can't be seen around DAMC, then what are you doing here? I'm one hundred percent DAMC. You know that."

Axel raised his palms up. "Hey, I'm just here for the cupcakes."

"Right," Bella scoffed. "You keep telling yourself that."

"And Dad wants me to keep an eye on Sophie."

Sophie's brows knitted. "Why?"

Axel lifted a shoulder. "I guess he wants to make sure things stay quiet around here."

"Things are quiet. If that's why you're always stopping by, then don't bother."

"Sophie..." he started.

"No, Axel. I don't need you 'taking care' of me, either."

"I'm not. I really love your cupcakes."

"So you keep saying."

"It's true."

Bella reached into the display case, snagged a Tiramisu cupcake and shoved it towards Axel. "There you go. Here's a fucking cupcake. Take it and go."

"Bella..."

"Bye," she said with a raise of her eyebrows, which clearly meant "get gone."

Axel looked at the cupcake in his hand. "Am I going to like this one?"

Bella blew out an impatient breath. "How the fuck would I know? Bye," she repeated.

Axel's lips flattened out. "Fine. I'll stop back during first shift tomorrow."

"Can't wait," Bella said and turned her back to him.

Axel looked toward Sophie, dug into the front pocket of his jeans and threw a crumpled five-dollar bill onto the counter by the register. "Thanks."

"You get two for five," Sophie said.

"I'll pick the second one up tomorrow."

She gave him a sharp nod, and he turned and left, looking a bit put out.

Sophie moved behind the display case and leaned against the counter watching Bella's stiff, jerky movements as she assembled more boxes.

"You don't have to do that. You're not a paid employee."

Bella's chest heaved as she took a deep breath. She turned and leaned a hip against the counter, mirroring Sophie. "I know. I just want to help out because I appreciate you doing this. You could've kicked me out when you did Z. Rid yourself of all of us. You know," Bella dragged a hand through her long, thick dark hair, "you're still at risk with me being here if the Warriors want retribution for whatever they're looking for retribution for. Which... who knows what the hell it's about this time. One could've gotten a hangnail and it would be DAMC's fault. This whole life can be fucked sometimes."

"Then why are you a part of it?" Sophie asked gently.

"Because it's my life. I don't know any different. They're my family. Always have been. I'm not going to desert my family when things get rough. I'm not going to do what Mitch and Axel did to Z. It's wrong."

Sophie pulled her bottom lip between her teeth. She agreed. But then, isn't that what she did to Zak also? Things got rough, and she kicked him out of her life.

"So what do you think of me, then?"

The blood drained from Bella's face at Sophie's question. "I didn't mean... Sophie, it's not the same. You didn't choose this. He sort of forced it on you. I don't blame you for doing what you did."

Her words did not make Sophie feel any better, though they should.

"He's a good guy, Sophie. He really is. He's always wanted what was best for the club, what was best for all of us. He sees better things for the club's future. As Ace always says, Zak's been progressive."

Sophie chewed on her bottom lip. "He's a misogynist."

Bella laughed, and Sophie was shocked at the beautiful tone of it. It brightened the whole shop. She couldn't help but smile at the sound.

"It's true!" Sophie insisted.

"No shit. Aren't they all? But let me tell you something, Sophie, all you have to do is get them wrapped around your little finger and they sing like a canary. They're not supposed to talk club business with their ol' ladies. But you think that Ace doesn't have pillow talk with Janice? You think Pierce doesn't talk things out with his woman? They need us. We give them a different perspective and they'll die before they admit it but they respect our opinions. Now... the house mouse or the sweet butt or the fuck... Hell, the strippers, the patch whores... the list goes on. They don't get told shit. A good man will respect his ol' lady. And don't be put off by the name either. Believe it or not, it's really a term of endearment. The rest of them... all those others hang out at the club, put out, clean up, do whatever they're told, just with the hopes of becoming an ol' lady. Sometimes it happens, most times it doesn't. They come and they go like the tides."

"Damn. I don't even know where to begin with my questions," Sophie mumbled.

Bella threw her head back and laughed again. And, once again, it pulled a smile from Sophie.

"Like house mouse. What the hell is that?"

"Something you'll never be. The only thing Z has wanted from you was to be his ol' lady."

"Why?"

Bella shook her head. "You'd have to ask him. He's hurting, Sophie. I know he is. He's stuck on you. I want to ask you to give him a chance, but I'll understand if you won't. Why the Warriors want to take him down or out, I don't know. But I do have to say it's not only him. While he was away, they would show up, pull some stuff and then ride off back to wherever they go."

While he was away. A nice way of putting his prison term.

Bella continued, "They shot at Diesel a few times. For a while there, they were determined to take out our enforcer, our club's Sergeant at Arms. I seriously thought I'd lose my cousin to a bullet. But, there's no way D or any of them will live their lives in fear. Though, I heard rumors Diesel took care of that particular threat." She raised her palms up. "Not sure how. Don't want to know, either. Especially when we have Axel sniffing around here."

"Something between you and Axel?"

"Nope," Bella answered way too quickly.

"Was something ever between you and Axel?" she asked, rephrasing the question.

"I'll say this. I had it rough for a while. I won't go into details right now, but let's just say Axel knows more about it then a lot of the members do."

"Why does he know more?"

Bella hesitated, then looked Sophie straight in the eye. "He's a first responder. And I don't want to talk about that part of my life any further. It's not because it's you, it'd be the same for anyone."

Sophie nodded. She wouldn't pry. If Bella ever wanted to talk about it, Sophie would listen. Bella was turning into a good friend and she wanted to be there for her.

"So back to Z," Bella said. "If it wasn't for the stuff that went down, would you give him a shot?"

"Honestly, I'm not sure being a biker's ol' lady is for me. Hell, I've never even been on the back of a motorcycle."

"Really?"

"Really."

"Weather warms up and your ass would be affixed to the back of his. Clubs aren't all bad, Sophie. We give back to the community when we can. It's one way we're accepted so we're not run out of town. The cops harass us sometimes. Sometimes we deserve it, sometimes we don't. Some of the town folk don't like the strip club, but hey," she shrugged, "it makes good money, so apparently someone from this town is showing up to tuck wrinkled dollar bills into G-strings. Dawg does his best to make sure his girls aren't selling themselves. That will get him shut down quicker than anything. And he makes sure they stay clean. No drugs. No prostituting. He takes care of them, believe it or not. The rest of the businesses, well, they're all respectable. Pierce isn't running guns out of the gun shop. Ace isn't accepting stolen goods in the pawn shop. The garage isn't a chop shop. And Crow's tattoo shop is licensed like it should be. Plus, Hawk and I make sure there aren't any minors sneaking into the bar. Everything's on the up and up."

"Like I said before... quite an enterprise."

"Yes, it is. And like I said before, we live good. We party, we drink, we laugh, we love. And we do it *hard*. Nothing's done half-assed. So, think about that when you're thinking about Z."

"Who said I'm thinking about Zak?"

Bella just gave her a smile and went back to assembling pastry boxes.

Shit.

Chapter Thirteen

SOPHIE TRIED to roll over but hit a brick wall instead. And part of that wall felt like it laid on her waist. Her hands grasped whatever it was... which was a hairy arm. And obviously it wasn't hers.

Her heart jumped and pounded fiercely as she lifted her head, trying to see the person behind her in the dark. She was definitely still in her own bed and, thank goodness, hadn't been knocked out and kidnapped, waking up in some strange room. But whoever it was had her pinned to him.

"What..."

A nose nuzzled her hair and she stiffened. She jerked against his arm but he didn't release her, instead tightening it around her waist, spreading the fingers of his hand along her lower belly. Low enough that a couple of his fingers were now below the elastic waist of her panties. She cursed at her body's response. Which was her pussy clenching and her nipples pebbling.

Fucking Zak.

A sound formed at the back of her throat when the fingers dipped lower, brushing the top of her narrow strip of hair. The clench turned into a throb.

But no matter how much her body wanted him, her brain said he shouldn't be here.

"How the hell did you not only get into my apartment but into my bed without me knowing? Are you a biker ninja? How did you get past the security system?"

"D gave me the code."

She closed her eyes at the roughness of his voice. She had missed its low rumble. But she needed to stay on track and not let her wanting him get in the way of staying on that track.

Diesel. When he'd finished installing the security system, she should have asked him to show her how to change the code and then changed it to something no one would know but her.

But she didn't. Her mistake.

And, now, that mistake was curled around her, his bare chest to her back, her ass to his groin, his knees cocked behind hers. His warm breath tickling the hair by her ear.

A shiver ran through her that turned to a quiver at her core when she felt him growing hard against her ass.

"You shouldn't be here," she whispered, cursing the catch in her voice.

"I know."

His fingers slid lower, his middle one separating her now slick folds to find her clit. He pressed gently.

"I… I told you to *get gone.*"

His body jerked slightly at her words. "I know, babe."

"But you're here."

"Couldn't stay away any longer." His words were so soft they were like a caress.

She needed to keep him out of her bed, out of her life. But when he pressed his face into her neck, his beard scraped her skin, his tongue traced a line along her jaw, she knew right then and there she was fucked.

And that she wanted fucked. Not just by anyone, but by the man who slipped into her bed in the middle of the night because he could no longer stay away.

She wanted this man who was not good for her. This man who may put her at risk, may put her business at risk.

She felt weak that she couldn't push him away, tell him to stop, scream at him to get out of her house, out of her life. Claw at his arms and hands until he let her go.

She didn't want him to let her go.

She wanted him to hold her tighter.

Which was crazy. Completely insane. In the last month, they spent less than a week together and then the rest of the time apart.

But she couldn't get him out of her head. Out of her restless dreams.

It seemed like he couldn't forget her, either.

At the moment, the way his fingers stroked her, teased her, pressed against her, made her hips dance, she was glad he hadn't forgotten her.

Though, she'd probably regret it tomorrow.

He rolled her to her back, his hand deep in her panties, making her think about nothing but him being inside her, until he murmured, "babe," against her skin and she completely melted.

He crushed his lips to hers and she opened to him willingly, the tips of their tongues touching as he explored her mouth, their tongues dancing, swirling, tangling, until she needed to pull away, gasp for breath when he rolled her nipple between his fingers, pulling hard, making her cry out.

"Zak," escaped her on a breath.

"That's right, babe, it's me, Zak." He sucked her bottom lip between his teeth and gently bit down, before releasing her and moving down the bed, down her body, worshiping her breasts, her belly, one hip, then the other. He tugged her panties down her thighs, over her knees, sliding them off her feet and tossing them into the darkness.

"I want to see you," he said, his voice rough, demanding, as he switched on the bedside lamp.

She squinted at the sudden light but studied the man who now straddled her hips, his body a work of art made up of both ink and muscle. His eyes were dark, his face hungry as he took her in, murmuring, "You're so beautiful."

Those words alone were beautiful coming from a man who was a badass biker who had spent the last ten years in prison.

He could be hard, but yet so soft, gentle. He cupped her breasts, stroking her nipples with his thumbs, then dropped his head until he could suck one deep into his mouth, flicking the tip, nibbling around the edge until she arched her back and dug her fingers into his hair, longer than it was a month ago, more to grab, more to pull. More to hold him where she wanted him.

With a quickness she wasn't expecting, he spread her thighs and settled between them. "Missed your sweet honey, babe." Then she heard nothing else as his hot mouth found her, his fingers slid deep, and he drew an orgasm from her that made her fist her hands in his hair, holding him close until it was over. Her body fell back onto the mattress, but he wasn't done with her yet.

Oh no. Nowhere near done.

He nipped her inner thighs, one then the other, then worked his way down to her ankles and back up the other side before flipping her over and doing it all over again, finally kissing, sucking and gently biting her ass cheeks, separating them, teasing her hole with the tip of his tongue, then moving up her spine. Finally, he pushed her heavy hair off her neck and bit the top of her spine as his cock nestled in the cleft of her ass. He rocked against her, tempting her to push back against him, to encourage him to take her there or her pussy. Hell, anywhere she could get him.

She felt him shift and heard his belt buckle jingle as he snagged his jeans off the floor to grab a condom.

"Can't wait, babe. You ready?"

Oh, fuck, yes, she was.

She shoved her face into her pillow and tilted her hips, and he accepted that as her answer. Within seconds, his cock was there, hard, hot, gliding between her soaked folds, asking for entry. She gladly gave it, digging her fingers into the pillow as he slowly drove deep. She wanted all of him and he gave it to her, thrusting hard enough to make her ass bounce with the force.

Then he stopped, yanked her hips back and up until she was on her knees, and without breaking the connection, he leaned over, dug into her nightstand and grabbed her small vibrator.

Her nipples hardened and ached at the hum of the toy. Reaching beneath her, he pressed it to her clit and began to move again. It took only seconds, milliseconds until she climaxed around him once more, her toes curling, her inner muscles squeezing him tight and he grunted, his hips hiccupping.

"Fuck, babe. Feelin' you come around me is sometimes better than my own release."

With a tighter hold on her hip, he moved to press the vibrator against her again, but she stopped him. "Too sensitive. Not there."

He stilled for a moment, then shifted once more to dig into the drawer. And when she heard the snap of the lube cap, she realized he understood what she wanted.

The cool liquid against her heated skin made her press her forehead deeper into her pillow and grasp the sheets tighter within her fingers. Then she felt it. The vibrations pulsating around her sensitive flesh.

"Yes, baby," she groaned.

"Fuck," came his strangled answer.

The vibrator was small and smooth and she accepted it easily. As he glided it in and out of her, he began to move again, slowly at first, then faster, softly at first, then harder.

"Beautiful, babe," he groaned. "So beautiful."

She moved with him, her body flowing with his as he took her once more to the cliff. She hovered until he pushed her over. She free fell, her core rippling around him blending with the vibrations of the toy. Her eyes rolled back, and she cried out his name.

"That's it, babe. That's it. Call my name," he grunted, his fingers digging into her hip, holding her tighter as he began to slam her harder, their skin slapping together, their sweat mingling.

And when she thought he was there, about to follow her over, he stopped, slipped the toy and himself from her. She glanced over her shoulder in surprise.

"On your back. Want to see you."

Good idea. Best idea ever. She wanted to see him when he came, too. She wanted to watch the pleasure overcome him, take him under.

She rolled over and reached out a hand. "Come to me, baby."

Something flashed behind his eyes and then he was there, inside her, curved over her body, thrusting hard, deep, making them one. He sucked a nipple into his mouth but his eyes remained tipped toward her face. And she didn't close hers, didn't look away, she kept her gaze locked to his. He smiled around her nipple and snagged the other between his fingers to twist. Her neck bowed and her mouth gaped, but she fought to hold his eyes. She desperately needed to stay connected in all ways.

"Come to me, baby," she pleaded again.

He did. Pressing his forehead to hers, they both lost focus, but didn't break their connection, their bond. With his lips a hair's breadth from hers he groaned, "Fuck, babe, gonna come."

"Yes... me, too. Come with me, baby."

"Fuck, Sophie. You're so hot, so wet. Wanna give you everything. Everything I have. Everything that is me. It's all yours, babe. I'm all yours."

His words swirled around inside her head as the orgasm began at her toes, landed in her core, and exploded outward around him.

"Comin' inside you now," he grunted. "Here I come, babe. *Ah... fuck.*" His body tensed as he stared into her eyes and drove deep one last time.

She gripped his ass, holding him tight against her as his cock pulsated inside her with the last of his release. Then he dropped as if he no longer had any strength and even though most of his weight was on her, she didn't mind. She didn't want him to move.

"Babe," he groaned. "Gotta move. Crushin' you."

"Stay," she whispered, raking the hair out of his face with her fingers, wiping beads of sweat off his forehead with her thumb.

He buried his face in her neck, tasting her damp skin, making little sounds against her that made her squeeze her pussy tight around his still-hard cock. "Can't do round two yet," he murmured.

Sophie smiled at the ceiling. Though she shouldn't since things just became more complicated again.

"Babe."

The whisper in her ear made her blink. The digital clock on her nightstand appeared blurry so she blinked again. 5:15.

He sucked her earlobe into his mouth and she felt that pull all the way to her toes.

"Babe," he whispered again in her ear.

"Yeah?" she whispered back, turning in his arms to face him. "What's the matter?"

He drew a finger along her brow, pulling her hair away from her face. Then he grabbed a handful of it in his fist and planted a kiss on her lips. He snagged her wrist with his fingers and pressed her hand to his erection.

"You do this to me," he murmured.

"Yeah," she breathed. "It's early."

"Yeah, gotta go."

"Now?"

"Yeah. Need to talk to you first," he said softly.

His face was unreadable, his eyes serious. Sophie's heart skipped a beat.

"Now?" she asked again.

"It's important."

She nodded, feeling the tug of her hair still in his grip. "Okay."

When he hesitated and his eyes searched her face in the early morning light, the blood rushed into her ears.

After last night, she had no idea what he was going to say. They had fallen asleep exhausted, sated, but with things unsettled.

Neither of them had wanted to ruin what they had with words, with the possibilities, or even the impossibilities.

And Sophie wasn't sure if she was ready to hear them now, either.

But Zak said it was important, so if it was important to him, it was important to her.

She realized at that moment that she not only lost her damn mind, she'd lost her heart.

To a badass, tattooed, ex-con biker. So not the *bring-the-boy-home-to-mom-and-dad* type. Not that he was a boy.

He proved time and time again that he was all man. The ache between her thighs from the hours they spent getting *down and dirty* reminded her of that.

He cupped her cheek and said, "Hear me out, 'kay?"

"Okay," she said again.

"Askin' for time, babe... Sophie. Askin' you to give it to me. I'll come after dark. Drive a car no one recognizes. Won't bring you to the clubhouse, won't tell anyone. Warriors won't tie you to me at all if that's your worry." His voice lowered. "Won't claim you. All I ask is you give me the same time I gave you. If after three weeks you don't want me, I'm not for you, then I'll respect that. You won't see me again. Promise you that." He traced a finger over her eyebrows, down her nose, over her lips. "You can have your days free of me. Just give me your nights. That's all I ask."

Then he got quiet. And she waited. When his eyes got a worried look, she realized he was waiting for her answer.

As she didn't know how to say what she felt, she asked him a question instead. "Bella know you're here? That you were coming to talk to me?"

Of course she knew. After their conversation in the bakery yesterday, she had no doubt that Bella said something to Zak. She didn't blame her. She'd known Zak her whole life. Bella only knew Sophie for a month. Her loyalties lay with the club members. Zak, especially.

"Yeah, she's the only one. Promise."

"My business can't be at risk. Neither can my life."

He blinked slowly, and then touched his nose to hers, murmuring, "Don't want to risk you, either. Don't think I can live without you."

All the oxygen left her lungs, her chest ached, her heart thumped all the way up into her throat.

"You don't know me, Zak," she whispered shakily.

"Keep tellin' you I know you." He pressed a flat palm to his heart. "Know you here."

Holy Hannah, he was killing her. "I don't know you, either."

"You do. But that's why I'm askin' for time. Take those three weeks, babe. Get to know me. You happy at the end, great. You're not... I'll go."

She studied him, he was trying desperately to hide his emotions. But she could see it. In his expression, in his eyes. That uncertainty was there. Here was a man who liked to take what he wanted, not have to ask, or even beg. This was going against the very fiber of his being.

This was costing him.

He wanted her that much.

And, goddamn, that ripped her in two. Tore at her heart, spun her mind.

And deep down, she suspected there was fear, though he'd never admit it. Fear that someone else wouldn't want him in their life.

Shit he had to deal with for most of his life since the day he decided to follow in his grandfather's footsteps. For most people, the family would see that as an honor. For his, not so much. In fact, not at all.

He took one fork in the road, his father and brother took the other. Which one would she follow? The question was, which one *should* she follow?

And once again, her heart and her head warred. "Three weeks?"

His nostrils flared and his body got tight as he anticipated her answer. "Yeah, babe. Just three."

"You got it. But you will honor my decision at that point."

His body relaxed, and a spark flashed in his eyes. "Yeah." He leaned closer, pressing their mouths together, touching the tip of his tongue to hers for a moment. Before it could intensify, he pulled away reluctantly, giving her a grin. "Now I gotta go."

He rolled from the bed, grabbing his clothes, quickly pulling them on. And as she watched him cover his body, shrug on his cut, she observed all that softness she just witnessed disappear as he became Z the badass biker, instead of Zak the thoughtful lover.

He leaned over the bed, pressed a kiss to her forehead, and whispered, "Tonight." Then he was gone.

Chapter Fourteen

AFTER THREE WEEKS, she didn't stop him from coming at night. After six weeks, she didn't turn him away, either. As promised, he disappeared during the day, doing whatever badass bikers did. Sometimes he'd sneak in around dinner just in time for her to make him a plate. Other times, he'd crawl into bed after midnight, smelling faintly of beer.

Never drunk, though. No.

And he never pushed her to make a decision. Not once.

Now it was warm enough, he wanted to take her out on his bike. But he refused to bring it to her place, to park it behind the bakery. He wouldn't risk it.

So the car he bought, the one no one knew was his, remained parked in the back lot, as they climbed into her car and he drove it to a storage unit about five miles out of town.

This, what he told her, was where he stored the car during the day, came and picked it up, swapping it out with that "piece of shit" he still borrowed from some brother named Crash, to drive over to her place every night. She was touched at the effort to keep her safe. To keep her from getting entangled in the club's "beefs."

But it was soon time to shit or get off the pot.

Either she wanted to be with him without hiding or she didn't.

Again, it wasn't something he pushed. However, it was something that gnawed at her.

He deserved better. Especially since his family treated him like a pariah. That ate at her, too. She didn't want to do the same thing.

So now, instead of driving the POS, he lived on his bike. When they parked her car in front of a unit, he unlocked the padlock and shoved the door up and open.

And there it sat. His pride and joy.

It was beautiful. Almost as beautiful as the man who rounded it, threw a leg over and then hit the starter.

The bike growled to a start and Sophie covered her ears because the echo of what he called straight pipes roared around her, amplified in the small concrete space. Though, he also told her, that space was bigger than the one he'd lived in for the last ten years.

He duck-walked the bike out of the storage unit and once it was out in the dark of the night, she could understand the appeal of what sat between his legs. She had to admit it was one hot, badass bike to match her hot, badass lover. The deep rumble vibrated through her all the way to her bones. Her blood began to rush at the rich sound and the look of satisfaction on Zak's face. He tilted his head back toward the unit and yelled over the exhaust.

"Lid, babe. Gotta wear it."

The helmet. He had explained, while he could go without, she couldn't. Not yet. And since she'd never been on the back of a bike before, she agreed it might be for the best.

"But once you feel that wind in your hair, babe, it'll be in your blood. So bear with the lid for now," he had said on the drive over.

After grabbing the full-faced helmet from inside the unit, she pulled it on, while he slipped on goggles. Then he helped her adjust the chin strap, making sure it was snug before holding an arm out for her to grab onto for balance as she climbed on behind him.

After tying one bandana around his head and one around his neck, he reached behind him, snagged her wrists and wrapped her arms around him tightly, saying, "Hold on as tight as you can, don't wanna lose you."

She didn't want to lose him, either. And she didn't mind hugging him close, pressing her now hard-tipped nipples into his back, skootching her crotch tight to his ass.

He reached back, squeezed her thigh and turned his head to say, "If you let it, the bike might get you off," before pulling the skull bandana from around his neck over his lower face.

What? What did he mean? How was that even possible?

There was no point in answering through the closed helmet, so she just nodded as if he made sense and then he took off.

After a few miles, the butterflies in her belly disappeared, and she relaxed enough to enjoy the ride.

It seemed they rode forever. Out into the dead of night, into the country, through a few small towns where the traffic was quiet, the residents asleep. But they weren't. They were wide awake, feeling alive, enjoying the warm weather, enjoying their close contact.

Now she understood his tattoo that read "Ride to live, live to ride." She could understand how it could get into your blood. The feeling of freedom, the power between your legs. She couldn't imagine him living without this for a decade.

The longer they rode, the more she became one with the bike and Zak, and then it hit her what he meant earlier, because she was hit with *it*. The rumble of the engine vibrated up between her thighs, making her throb, making her want him badly. But they were too far out, and she doubted he would pull over or that they could find a private spot to take care of her needs. So she squeezed her eyes shut, pressed her helmet to his back harder, and slipped her hands lower until she cupped him tight. He dropped one hand to hers as she began to rub him through his jeans, feeling him grow beneath her fingers, until she panted in her helmet, steaming up the face shield.

Then it hit *her*.

The orgasm ripped through her and she cried out, her fingers clenching around him, making him tense.

The bike swerved as he pulled off into the parking lot of a closed park, brought the bike to an abrupt halt, kicked down the kickstand and jumped off, ripping down the bandana from his face. He tugged her helmet's straps loose and pulled it from her, setting it on the ground.

Then he grabbed her face in both hands and kissed her hard, crushing his mouth to hers, making her groan down his throat.

"*Fuck*, babe."

"It happened," she said, still a little surprised it did.

"I know. Harley's the best an' biggest vibrator out there."

"That's for damn sure."

"Now you got me worked up," he said, rubbing his fingers over his bulging zipper.

"What are we going to do about it?"

He glanced around the lot. Since it was the middle of the night and the park was officially closed, the place was empty. "Always wanted to fuck on my bike."

Sophie's eyes widened. She'd never had sex in a public place. Never even had sex outside. And definitely not on the back of a bike.

"How far are we away from home?"

"Way too far."

"I was afraid of that. Is it doable?" she asked, hoping it was.

Funny that he understood exactly what she meant. "Yeah," his voice rumbled deep from within his chest, sort of like the bike's straight pipes. "Get off the bike."

When she hesitated, because she was trying to figure out in her head how they were going to pull it off, he said, "Off. Now. Hurry."

She bit her bottom lip trying not to giggle at his impatience.

"Next time, you're wearin' a short skirt so you can ride me while I'm still on the bike."

She didn't think a short skirt was very smart to wear on a bike. In fact, she would probably end up flashing all her goodies to everyone as they rode. But she'd argue that point later. They had some other urgent business to attend to first.

"Pants an' panties to your knees. Now."

At the same time she was scrambling to do as she was told, he was pushing his jeans down far enough to frame his hard-on, then ripping a condom out of his big-assed leather and chain wallet to roll it on.

"Hands on the seat. Stretch your arms an' ass out. Careful of the pipes, the engine. They'll burn you. Serious, babe. Gimme your ass, keep your legs away."

Just the heat rolling off the bike made it clear how serious a burn she would get if she touched any hot metal with her bare flesh. She bent over, planted her hands on the seat and pushed out, offering herself to him.

And within seconds... he took her. Hard, fast, rough, fingers digging into her hips, hips slapping against her ass, grunting with every stroke as he fucked her from behind. She couldn't come like this but she'd already had her climax. Now it was his turn. But he reached around her and touched her where she needed it the most, where the vibrations from the engine had made her most sensitive.

Almost as fast as their first night together months ago, they both came, tensing and crying out at the same moment, their bodies releasing and pulsing together. They stayed connected until the aftershocks stopped and their breathing slowed. Then he bent over, placed a kiss above her ass and slipped out of her. He disposed of the condom in a nearby receptacle, pulled up his jeans, and when he returned to the bike, he said, "Let's ride."

Yes, she thought, let's. She never would have guessed that riding on the back of a motorcycle could be so satisfying.

Now she was cluing in on why so many women hung around the club, hung around these men. She didn't blame them one bit.

"Babe, you just made ridin' my Harley so much sweeter," he said over his shoulder. "Thank you for that."

She smiled, pulled on her helmet, and wrapped her arms around her man. "You're welcome."

He chuckled, shook his head, yanked his bandana back up, pulled down his goggles, and off they went.

Shit or get off the pot. It was a decision she had avoided for over six weeks. And she couldn't jerk him around any longer.

Tonight made her realize that she either had to give him his freedom or step into the role of being his ol' lady. See and be seen. Have his back. Or let him live his life and let him find someone else who could do just that.

As they rode back into the night, she knew her decision had already been made.

Chapter Fifteen

Zak pulled the bike to the front of the bakery. Sophie could see Bella inside waiting on a customer. It was nice to have her there full-time now, her first actual paid employee. It gave her time to do silly stuff like this... Go to lunch on the back of a badass Harley with her badass, but freaking hot, biker boyfriend.

He planted his boots on the pavement, backed the bike to the curb and kicked the stand down.

She slipped off her helmet aka brain bucket. Yes, she had her very own now. A badass black one with a tinted face shield so she could go incognito. Not that she needed to. They hadn't been hiding their relationship for the last month.

And so far, everything was quiet in Shadow Valley, for the most part.

Well, except for the wild-assed pig roasts, and parties that happened way too often. So often, that most times they didn't even show up at the clubhouse for them, preferring the quiet of her apartment. Well, not so quiet when he had her screaming with orgasms. Not to mention, his grunting could get a little loud.

A smile curved her lips.

The sex was hot, her man was hot, and the business at the bakery was picking up. She might even have to hire a second employee soon.

"You gonna sit back there an' daydream or you gonna get your sweet ass off an' get to makin' me one of those chocolate cakes with those chocolate curly things on the top?"

Her man had a sweet tooth. He especially loved anything chocolate. But then, that shouldn't have surprised her since his brother did as well.

Though, now she was pretty sure Axel was sweet on Bella, too.

"We going to the party tonight?" she asked him as she dismounted the bike, trailing her fingers along the back of his neck as she did so.

"Band's gonna be there," he said as he got off the bike and stood next to it.

"Dirty Deeds?"

"Yeah."

Well, there was her answer. They'd be at least hitting the party for a couple hours. Nash, one of the brothers, played the drums and sometimes sang in the AC/DC cover band and whenever they played one of the roasts or parties, most of the brothers showed up. At least, the ones that weren't working or doing security at the strip club or The Iron Horse. They usually set up a camera with a live feed into the bar so the patrons could enjoy the music, too. But they made sure the lens only focused closely on the band and not some of the debauchery that happened out in the courtyard. Like the head jobs by the fence given by some of the "sweet butts," the biker groupies who wanted to be more than just that. Or the sex that happened on the picnic tables under the open pavilion. And some of that could get pretty creative.

Sophie got used to seeing it, so now she ignored it. Mostly. Sometimes she dragged Zak upstairs to his room at the clubhouse when he least expected it. He certainly didn't go up the steps kicking and screaming like she did that first night. No, he was usually laughing and murmuring about the dirty things he was going to do to her which encouraged her to go faster.

He took her into his arms, grabbing her ass and squeezing while he planted a kiss on her lips. Then he smacked her ass hard before letting her go.

"Want me to pick you up later?" he asked.

"Nope. I'll drive over. I'll bring some goodies to the party."

"Some of the brothers are gonna try to steal you away if you keep doin' that."

"I know. That's why I do it. To keep you on your toes," she teased, smiling up at him.

His eyes flashed as he smiled back at her. "No one else's goin' to taste any of your sweet honey. *My* sweet honey."

"Just you?"

"Just me, babe." He gave her a gentle push. "Now get that sweet ass of yours back inside. Bella's starin' at us."

As Sophie turned to look in the large front picture window, Zak yelled, "God-fucking-damnit!" which made her freeze and her head spin back around. What happened next took seconds but felt like it happened in slow motion.

A motorcycle sped up the street, the biker's face covered in a black bandana, dark goggles, and a black leather skull cap as he closed in towards Sophie standing by Zak's bike. She watched in dismay as his arm snaked out to snag her. Zak was faster, pegging the guy's body with the bottom of his boot and putting all his weight behind it.

The biker lost his balance, Sophie jumped back, the bike skidded out from underneath the guy who rolled into the middle of the street.

A black handgun skittered across the pavement, across the two lanes of travel before sliding to a stop along the curb.

Before the motorcycle and its rider came to a complete stop, Zak was running, leaping over the downed bike and landing on top of the guy, pounding the shit out of him, kneeing the guy in the gut, slamming the other man's head into the pavement. Over and over.

Sophie felt like her feet were stuck in concrete. She couldn't breathe, she couldn't scream, she couldn't move. Watching Zak violently pound the other biker made it worse. She'd never seen him this out of control before.

And never wanted to again.

Bella came running out of the shop, cursing, coming to an abrupt stop in the middle of the street, just feet from them, eyes wide. "What the fuck!"

"Call Diesel," Zak shouted to her as he slammed the guy's skull one more time into the pavement.

"I'm calling Axel," Bella shouted back.

"Call Diesel, Bella!" Zak shouted even louder, his impatience clear.

"No! I'm calling Axel!" She rushed back onto the sidewalk and closed in on Sophie, her hands shaking as she jabbed a finger at her cell. She mumbled, "This needs to stay on the up and up." Cell to her ear, she said, "Axel? Yeah. Hey—" Then Bella stepped back inside the shop.

Sophie realized she hadn't moved an inch. Still frozen in place, she was unable to peel her eyes from the scene before her.

She shook herself mentally. She had to do something before Zak killed the other biker. "Zak!" she screamed.

He ignored her, giving the guy a solid punch to the jaw. The guy's head flopped to the side. He was out and no longer a threat. He needed to stop.

"Zak!" she screamed, running to where Zak straddled the unconscious man. "Don't kill him! Jesus! You'll end up back in prison!"

Zak froze, his fist cocked back, the skin on his knuckles broken and bleeding. He twisted his head to look at her, his eyes wild, chest heaving. "Sophie," he said almost in a trance.

"Is he out?" Of course, the guy was out. She just wanted him to recognize that fact.

He dropped his gaze to the man beneath him. "Yeah."

"Let him be." Her eyes flicked to the gun still in the street across from them. "Get the gun."

There was no way she was picking it up. She knew nothing about weapons, and the last thing she needed was to accidentally shoot someone by handling it.

Zak pushed to his feet, then gave the Warrior a boot to the ribs for good measure. "Can't touch the gun, Sophie. They'll throw me back into that hell quicker than shit if I do."

They couldn't just leave it there lying in the street. There was a crowd gathering, and the cars were skirting around them since they were blocking one lane of the street.

"Bella!" she screamed, and the woman rushed back out of the

bakery, pulling her phone from her ear and disconnecting. She pointed. "Gun."

Bella's eyes flew to where she pointed. "Fuck," she muttered. "Don't touch it. Could be stolen."

Well, then it was just going to remain where it was until law enforcement arrived. Her attention went back to her man. "Zak... Come here, baby," she pleaded, a hand outstretched, wanting to get him away from the biker before he decided to change his mind and do more damage. His gaze bounced from her to the downed biker back to her.

He approached the Warrior's bike which laid on its side against the curb and turned the key, cutting the engine. He jerked the keys out and whipped them down the street as hard as he could. As he approached where she and Bella now stood on the sidewalk, he asked Bella, "5-0 comin'?"

Bella only nodded, her expression worried.

"Fuck," he muttered. He turned to Sophie, his expression strangely void of any emotion. "Maybe you *should* go back to Philly. Club will help you with your expenses since it's club business that caused all this."

Her heart seized in her chest. "What? You convinced me to stay. I don't want to leave now. I'm not letting them," she jabbed a finger toward the downed biker, "run me out of my business."

"Babe."

"No, Zak. No more about that right now." Her eyes flicked toward the people gathering. "You need to get out of here?"

"Can't run, babe." He lifted his chin towards the crowd. "Too many eyes. Need to stay an' face whatever happens."

"You had a good reason."

"Right," he answered, then looked up the street.

She heard what he saw. Sirens, racing engines. Then they were there, parking at an angle to block the street, lights flashing.

Sophie lost her breath and her stomach dropped as doors flew open, guns were drawn. She watched in horror as Zak automatically dropped to his knees and laced his fingers behind his head.

What!

"Cross your ankles," one of the officers barked, pointing his gun at Zak. He complied immediately, his jaw tight, his eyes avoiding Sophie. The other officer, also a gun in hand, went to check on the unmoving Warrior.

Sophie was unsure what to do, unsure what to say.

The cop squatting by the injured biker, reached up to the radio mic on his shoulder. "Dispatch, get a bus en route. Code three. We got one subject down, one in custody."

As the first officer closed in on Zak, Sophie shouted, "He was only protecting me. The guy tried to grab me. He had a gun."

The cop ignored her, slapping cuffs on Zak's wrists. "Get up." He yanked Zak up by his arms. Zak got to his feet and twisted his neck toward Bella.

"Bella, this is what happens when you fuckin' call Axel. Call Diesel. Take Sophie to church an' keep her there 'til you hear otherwise. Fuckin' do as I say this time."

Bella, pale, nodded.

"That's enough," the cop barked, walking Zak to the car and with a hand to the top of his head shoved him into the back, slamming the door shut. Then he approached Sophie with a notebook and pen in hand.

"That's Mitch Jamison's son. He was only trying to protect me."

"Ma'am, I know who he is. I need your information. And yours, too," he said to Bella.

"Are you going to arrest him?"

"He's in custody right now until we get this all sorted out."

"I want to talk to Mitch or Axel," Sophie demanded.

The officer, whose name tag said Miller, nodded. "I'll let them know."

That didn't make Sophie feel any better. But she cooperated and gave him all her info and Bella did, too.

Sophie fought back the tears as the cop drove away with Zak in the back. It was made worse when Zak didn't look back at her, instead keeping his face forward.

"Will he go back to prison because of this?" she asked Bella as the ambulance arrived. As did Mitch in another cruiser. Followed quickly by Axel in his personal vehicle.

"I don't know," Bella whispered, her voice sounding as shaky as hers. "Fucking hope not."

She squeezed Bella's arm. "You did the right thing."

"No, I just got your old man arrested. *Fuck.*" Bella turned and headed back toward the bakery. When Axel rushed after her, she spun around, had some low, angry words with him that Sophie couldn't hear, then Bella slammed both palms into his chest, shoving him off the stoop of the bakery.

Oh shit.

He caught his balance, grabbed her arm and yanked her inside, slamming the front door behind them, hard enough that the large picture window even rattled.

Sophie thought it might be better to stay outside and talk to Mitch, who stood watching everything that just transpired also, eyebrows knitted and a deep frown on his face.

Fuck.

She turned to Mitch and began to plead Zak's case.

"Was only protectin' my woman," Zak mumbled as his father stepped into the room where he was being held. Mitch's eyes were hard, and he looked pissed.

He couldn't be more pissed than Zak, though. He'd been sitting here for hours, unable to leave even after giving his statement. Being treated like the criminal everyone at the station thought he was. Including his own father.

What-fucking-ever.

"Sophie already went to bat for you. Explained everything. Axel heard the same story from Bella. Once we finish getting statements from witnesses who'd have no reason to lie, we'll get this all sorted out."

They needed to hurry up and get it sorted. He needed to check on Sophie. Bella had better have listened and taken her back to church where she'd be protected until they figured out what the fuck was going on with the Warriors.

"They didn't lie. He fuckin' tried to grab Sophie an' I kicked his ass. Had a damn gun."

"We recovered the gun."

"Stolen, wasn't it?" Zak asked, narrowing his eyes at Mitch. When his father didn't answer, he said, "Knew it would be. Serial numbers probably wiped. He coulda killed her. Killed me. Maybe even Bella. Then drove right outta town. An' all you *blue avengers* woulda been scramblin' to find who did it. Buncha bumblin' boys in blue," he spat, trying to get a rise out of the man who sired him. "Can't figure out who done the real crime." He wanted to remind his own flesh and blood that he'd been wrongly convicted. Not that the man probably cared.

Mitch's jaw hardened, his blue eyes turned a shade of steel, but he ignored the taunting, to Zak's disappointment.

The older man pointed a finger at Zak. "You need to leave her be, boy. But you won't listen. You never do, never had. Maybe if you had, you wouldn't have a felony conviction on your record right now. Plus, wouldn't be sitting here now secured to the wall like a dog."

A muscle ticked in Zak's jaw and he ground his teeth before grumbling, "Shit happens."

"Shit happens," Mitch repeated, shaking his head. He jammed his hands on his hips, his mouth tight. "Your mother loves you and it killed her when you went to Fayette."

"Why didn't she visit, then?"

His father's chest expanded when he sucked in a deep breath. "Because I wasn't going to let her see her son like that."

"What about you, Mitch?"

He winced when Zak called him by his first name. "What about me?"

"You still feelin' the fatherly love? Didn't see your ass during visitin' hours. Hell, you're law, you could've come at any hour."

His father's lips flattened and his mouth got tight again.

"Right," Zak continued, "I get not bringin' Jayde. But you, Axel, Mom." He shook his head. "You believe I did that shit? Had that shit?"

"Doesn't matter what I believe. You were convicted, Zakary. You were found guilty. Guilty or not, you put yourself in that position the moment you patched into that fucking club. I told you not to do it. I told you it would fuck up your life. You did it anyhow. I only ever wanted what was best for you and you fucking spit in my face. That's what you did."

Zak's head jerked back, and he pushed to his feet, the metal ring he was cuffed to clanging against the steel bracelet. Chained like a damned, dangerous animal.

By his own blood, too.

"Unless you're here to set me free, *cop*, get the fuck outta my face."

"Zak..."

Zak tightened his jaw and looked away, shaking his head.

He heard a strangled noise and when he looked up, his blood was leaving him still restrained to the wall.

"Fuck you, *Dad*," Zak yelled down the hallway at his father's retreating back. He sank back onto the metal bench, and dragged his free hand through his hair and down over his face, finally covering his mouth so he wouldn't beg his father to come back.

Chapter Sixteen

"FUCKER'S GOTTA report to his parole officer first thing tomorrow, but he's out!" Diesel bellowed as the back door whipped open so hard that it slammed the wall. A bunch of stomping, hooting and hollering followed that announcement.

Sophie spun on the bar stool where she sat with Bella, Jag, Crash, and Hawk, then jumped to her feet.

He had been released? She breathed with relief.

Once Diesel's large body veered off, she couldn't miss Zak coming in behind him, a grin on his face. He raised his hands and shrugged like there had been no doubt he'd be set free.

Right. Cocky.

She hadn't been the only one worried that he'd end up back behind bars. Everyone else who sat with her for the past few hours had worried about that, too.

Diesel made his way over to Pierce, who was shooting pool in the far corner, and bumped shoulders with him, dipping his head and talking low. Pierce nodded his head, whacked Diesel on the back and then took his shot, sending one of the balls careening across the table into the corner pocket.

Sophie wondered what that was about. Maybe she didn't want to know.

Her eyes shot back to Zak who had stopped in the middle of the large room, just standing there staring at her.

What was he waiting for?

"Waitin' on you, babe," he yelled, his grin getting bigger, his arms open in invitation.

Oh.

Hawk chuckled next to her. "Your man's waitin' on you. Go."

Oh!

What started as a fast walk turned into a fast jog and she didn't stop until her body hit his and he wrapped his arms around her, grabbing her ass and lifting her off her feet before shoving his face into her hair, breathing her in. "Fuck," he murmured near her ear.

He felt good in her arms, solid, safe. She swiped at her cheeks. "I was scared."

"Yeah," he whispered against her lips before kissing her. She slid back to her feet, but neither wanted to let go. "You don't go anywhere without me, without one of the prospects, or one of D's guys. At least until we find out what's goin' down. Got me?"

"Yeah," she said softly. "The bakery?"

"There, too. For now. Need to find out what the fuck's goin' on."

She nodded. She didn't like it but she realized it was for the best.

And she'd allow it. For now.

But she wasn't going to live like this forever, constantly worrying that someone was out to get her or Zak.

He hung his arm around her shoulders and guided her back to the bar where he clasped arms and bumped shoulders with Hawk, Crash, and his cousin, Jag.

Murmurs of "Good to see you out, brother," "Good job kickin' that fucker's ass," and more, rose around them and Bella poured him a draft, sliding the pint glass in front of him.

Their eyes met, and Bella murmured, "Sorry."

Zak shook his head. "You did right."

"Got you in a jam."

"Got out of it, thanks to your statement..." He squeezed Sophie's shoulders. "And Sophie's."

"Axel help?" Bella asked.

The corner of Zak's mouth twitched. "He did what he could."

"Meaning nothing."

Zak took a sip of his beer, then sighed. "Let it go."

Bella nodded her head, her eyes troubled, and said softly, "Love you, Zakary."

"Love you, too, Isabella."

She nodded again, managing a small but sad smile. Sophie knew Bella felt guilty and wished she could ensure her that it wasn't her fault.

Sophie snaked her arm under Zak's cut and around his waist, giving him a squeeze. His eyes dropped to her.

"Sorry for all the shit, babe."

She didn't know what to say to that. She couldn't answer, "It's okay," because it wasn't. None of it was okay.

But when she finally made the decision a few weeks ago to be with him, *really* be with him, she knew she might be stepping into some of the club's shit. Zak had never hidden that possibility.

"Can we go home now?"

"My sled here?" Zak asked Hawk.

"Rig flat-bedded it back," Crash said from two stools down. "Lucky that asshole's sled didn't take yours out."

"Yeah," Zak murmured, rubbing the back of his neck.

Sophie's eyes followed his movement, and she gasped. "Let me see your wrist."

Zak stilled, but Sophie reached up and snagged his arm, pulling it down so she could take a good look at the marks left behind from the cuffs. They had tightened them to the point of rubbing the skin raw.

"Ain't nothin', babe."

"That isn't nothing! They hurt you." She flipped his hand over and looked at his bruised, swollen knuckles that still had dried blood stuck to them in spots. She swallowed hard. "Damn it."

Zak tugged his hand from her and grumbled, "Ain't nothin'. Stop fussin'," then took another sip of beer.

Stop fussing? Sophie's brows rose then dropped as her eyes narrowed. Oh, no. He did *not* just say that. "Are we going?"

"Might be better if we crash here tonight."

"I'm not staying here. You want to stay here, you stay. I'm heading home. You want to come, fine. You want to send someone else with me, fine. They can sleep on the couch."

Now Zak's eyes narrowed. "No other man's sleepin' on your couch, woman."

Woman? "Then say your goodbyes and let's go," she said firmly.

Hawk snorted, Crash chuckled, and Jag blew out a loud breath in an attempt not to laugh.

"Sounds just like an ol' lady, brother," Pierce said coming up behind Zak and slapping him on the back. "Got your balls in a grip already."

His comment made her realize that she just cut Zak off at the knees in front of his brothers. Which was not good. He had talked to her many a night about how he wanted to take the president's spot back, and her emasculating him in front of the other members would not help his cause.

She bit her bottom lip recognizing her error. *Shit.*

Not putting up with his misogynist bullshit behind closed doors was one thing. Doing it in front of everyone else was another. She needed to back pedal and fast.

She forced her body to relax and her expression to soften. "Sorry, baby, I'm a little uptight about you getting arrested. Can we go home now?"

Zak's head swung back to her and his eyebrows lowered, clearly wondering about the sudden change in attitude.

She slid a hand up his chest and leaned into his hip. "I need some loving."

His eyebrows suddenly shot to the moon.

Pierce laughed and pounded him on the back again. "Go. Take care of your woman's needs. Meetin' tomorrow right after you meet with your P.O. Be here. I'll send Abe over in the mornin' so someone's with Bella an' her."

Zak nodded, grabbed her arm firmly and tugged her toward the door. "Let's go."

When they got outside, he loosened his grip, pulled her into his arms, dropped his mouth to hers and said, "Someone's gettin' a fuckin' spankin'. Guaranteed."

Sophie smiled. "Can't wait."

Zak laughed, intertwining his fingers with hers as they walked to her car. "Me, neither."

ZAK DUG his fingers into her hips as Sophie rose and fell on him. He was splayed out on his back and she straddled him, her pussy that he swore was lined with hot silk squeezed him tight.

He couldn't help but watch her face as she rode him, her mouth slightly open as little mews escaped, her eyes unfocused, her hair swinging, her full tits bouncing. Her dusky nipples hard as diamonds under his thumbs.

Fucking heaven.

Suddenly, she grabbed his wrists and slammed them to the mattress over his head and ground her hips in circles. She dropped her head, snagging one of his nipples between her teeth and he jerked in surprise.

"My fuckin' woman's wild," he said between gritted teeth, his balls tight, his brain about to explode from the torturous pleasure she was putting him through.

She circled her hips again, throwing her head back, jamming those luscious tits toward his face, but not close enough where he could pull one into his mouth. Damn, so close.

Then he felt it. That telltale ripple that meant she was about to come all over his dick. This woman could get slicker than shit, wetter than a Slip-n-Slide. But he was not complaining. No way. He loved it. Feeling that always drove him to the point where he couldn't hold back and had to bust a nut deep inside her.

Now that she was on the pill, he could do just that. There was nothing between them anymore. Just her hot, pulsating flesh surrounding his dick.

He slammed his head back into the pillow and jerked his hips up as she smashed her hot flesh down on him again.

"Fuck, babe," he grunted.

"You like that?" she asked, breathless.

"Oh... fuck... yeah."

She ground her hips against him again. "And that?"

"Fuck," he groaned.

She nipped his other nipple.

"Fuck!" he shouted.

"Yeah, baby... those are mine," she said before sinking her teeth into his neck.

Damn, his woman had been getting bossy in bed lately. Good thing he liked it or she would need a little attitude adjustment. Like last night when he spanked both her ass until it was red and her pussy until it was dripping. He had to admit his endurance had been tried after that. It didn't take them long to both come and then collapse into each other's arms.

He brought his attention back to the here and now. Which was Sophie doing the bump and grind on top of him.

But he didn't have to think about that long, because as soon as she grabbed her own tits, played with her own nipples, she arched her back and yelled that she was coming.

Thank fuck.

She squeezed his cock tight, pulsating around him until he blew his load deep inside her. After a few seconds she slowed and stopped, blowing out a breath, brushing her damp hair away from her face and she gave him a lazy smile, looking down at him with her sexy *just-been-fucked* eyes.

"Ready?" she asked, meaning: was he ready for her dismount? *Which* he wasn't. *Which* he couldn't think of anything better than being connected to her.

Which made him think of the meeting at church earlier in the day. *Which* was the last thing he should be thinking about while his woman was sitting on his cock.

Which made him realize he needed to talk to her. *Which* totally fucking sucked.

But his answer regrettably was, "Yeah."

She groaned as she rolled off him, and he groaned at the loss. He watched her naked hips swing as she went to the bathroom to clean up. Coming back a couple minutes later, she tossed a damp washcloth to him. He caught it, took care of business, tossed it to the floor—which she hated—then patted the bed for her to lay down next to him.

Not that there was any doubt that she'd climb into his arms afterward. She always did. His woman liked to cuddle.

And not that he'd admit this, even under the threat of death, he loved to snuggle with her, too.

Nothing like laying in the arms of a woman who loved him after she just drained his nuts dry.

Yeah, he knew she loved him. She hadn't said it... yet. But he knew. That's why he didn't look forward to bringing up what he needed to bring up.

But until things were sorted with what was going down with the Warriors, she was at risk. And he didn't like it. No, he fucking *hated* it. And it pissed him off to no end that she could be the target of some asshole who still felt as if he needed revenge for the four Warrior nomads Rocky and Doc took out over thirty years ago. And they had this mistaken idea that the DAMC would curl up like a ball and roll out of Shadow Valley, leaving it to them, if push came to shove. They needed to be corrected of that notion.

The Warriors could push all they wanted, DAMC would shove back harder.

Not the best plan since they were striving to remain legit. And the last thing any of them wanted was for more brothers to end up at Fayette. Or even Greene. But right now that was all they had.

They needed to take a stand.

"Baby?"

He turned his head at her whisper. "Yeah?"

"You have smoke coming out of your ears because you're thinking so hard."

He rolled to his side, cupping her cheek. “Sorry, babe, know you hate when I smoke.”

When a burst of laughter came out of her, it became infectious and he laughed with her, loving how her eyes sparkled when she was happy. Loved it when he’d catch her studying him and her eyes went soft and a small smile curved her lips. The first time he saw that, he knew.

He knew their lives would be entangled for a very long time. If not forever. As long as they could keep the Warriors—and the fucking cops—off their back.

Unfortunately, at today’s meeting, there was also mention of the Dark Knights making a play for more territory. They currently controlled area on the south side of the Burgh. But word was their club was outgrowing their area and wanted more. Which might mean they could want to spread closer to Shadow Valley. But they were currently at war with another club in that area, so for now, the DAMC had to wait to see how that all played out. Though, Zak thought Pierce needed to keep a finger on the pulse of that mess, be proactive, the sitting president didn’t think it was something to worry about. Yet.

Zak didn’t think Hawk, the club’s VP, would let something like that roll over the club without warning. But he needed to pull Hawk aside and get a read on how he thought Pierce was handling it.

Zak was pretty sure Hawk wasn’t on board with just letting things “play out” with the Dark Knights and whatever move they might make to expand.

“Baby.”

“Yeah?”

“I’m going to start choking on all that smoke.”

He chuckled and pressed his lips briefly to her forehead. He couldn’t imagine anything happening to her. It would kill him.

So there was no time like the present to rip off that damn Band-Aid. He had to do it quick and keep the pain to a minimum. He sucked in a breath. “You sure you don’t want to go back home, babe? It’d be safer for you. You want, Bella can run the bakery for you ‘til all this shit blows over.”

“I told you I’m not leaving. I’m not going to let them chase me away. And we don't know how long it's going to be until it all 'blows over.' It could be months."

Zak didn't want to tell her it might be years. Maybe even never. At least, not until the last Dirty Angel or Shadow Warrior was dead and buried.

Or, at least, until they came to some sort of understanding. But, again, Zak didn't think that would ever happen with Pierce at the gavel. And there were plenty of others in their midst who didn't want a truce, either. Too much bad blood between the clubs over the years.

"What happened at the meeting?"

He dipped his chin. "Babe."

"Don't *babe* me. Talk to me. Anybody find out anything?"

With a sigh, he said, "Not much. Some chatter, nothing solid."

"They targeting you in particular?"

"Dunno that, babe."

"So, what *do* you know?"

"Nothing concrete."

"Is this how it's going to be? You hiding club business from me? Even if it may affect me or my bakery?"

"Tellin' you what I can, Soph."

"But not what you know."

"Babe."

Sophie sighed. She rolled over and went nose to nose with him. "Tell me this... You're going to stay out of those steel bracelets, right? Not do anything stupid?"

"That's my plan."

"You going to fuck me whenever I want?"

"Not even a question."

"You going to work on grabbing that gavel back so this club of yours stays above board?"

"Yeah."

"You going to try to reconcile with your family?"

He had no idea where she was going with this line of questioning and he'd found it a bit amusing until the last question.

He frowned. "Can't promise you that."

"You going to love me for the rest of your life?"

His nostrils flared. He closed the slight gap between them, pressing his nose to hers. "You gonna wear my cut?"

THERE WAS no way Sophie would ever wear one of those "property of" vests. But she had talked at length with Bella about it. And Bella had given her a good idea. "No. But I might do something better."

He cocked an eyebrow. "What?"

"Can't tell you yet." See? Two could play at that game.

"Really."

"Really," she confirmed. "You didn't answer my question."

"Which one?"

"Zakary Jamison, are you going to love me 'til death do we part?"

"Need more details than that."

She pulled away from him and gave him a look. "Like what?"

"You askin' for it to be legal?"

Yes. "Maybe."

"Kids?"

Oh yes. "Possibly." But first there would have to be a lengthy discussion about raising them around the club. She wasn't sure if she wanted that yet, though they had plenty of time to decide. She wanted to make sure her bakery was well-established before having a baby hanging on her hip.

"Babe, no 'maybe' or 'possibly' about it. Just tellin' you now."

This man of hers not only wanted to marry her but wanted kids. This badass biker wanted to bounce a baby on his knee. She smiled at the image. "So... is that a yes?"

"To what?"

She shoved him and he landed on his back with her on top of him, staring down into his face. "Just so you know, I'm not going to stand behind you, I'm going to stand beside you."

"We'll see." He pressed his lips together to keep from smiling. He was messing with her now. But not a second later, he got serious, "You wanna be my ol' lady, huh?"

She wasn't thrilled with that term, but... "Well, am I a house mouse?"

"No."

"Am I a sweet butt?"

"Fuck no."

"Then what other choice do I have?"

He tucked a strand of hair behind her ear, then slid his hands down her back to grab her ass tight. "Never had another choice."

She rolled her eyes. "No shit."

"Babe, the minute... no, the second I saw you I knew I wasn't goin' to let you say no."

"Even if I *was* kicking and screaming."

He grinned. "Yeah, I fucked up. Or so I thought. Turned out to be a blessin' in disguise, though. Yeah?"

"Yeah," she echoed softly.

"Gotta tell you somethin', Sophie."

Oh, boy, now what? "What?"

"Love you more than my freedom. An' after losin' it, that's sayin' somethin'."

It certainly was. Her lungs emptied with a whoosh and her heart swelled. But it was his next words that made her want to cry.

"You're my breath, Sophie. My life's blood. You're my soul."

How did this happen? How did any of this happen? Her life wasn't supposed to go this direction, but it did.

At first, she thought she'd regret it.

Now, she knew she didn't.

"So, you got me, babe?"

She swiped at her eyes and gave him a smile. "Got you."

"Love me?"

"Love you," she said with a nod. Her vision became blurry, and she tried to blink the tears away.

It was a losing battle.

"Now who's talkin' in two-word sentences?"

She laughed through the tears. "You're a bad influence, Zak Jamison."

"That I am."

"Will there be a problem with your brothers if I don't wear your cut?"

"Only wear it if you wanna, babe. But I think everyone knows you're mine."

"That they do." She cupped his cheeks and pressed her forehead to his. "Love you, Zak."

"Love you, babe."

Epilogue

Sophie didn't know everything about motorcycle clubs, not yet anyway, but she figured most MCs weren't diverse, meaning: like stuck to like. To see Crow's coloring surprised her.

But he was one hell of a beautiful man. His sharp facial features combined with his light caramel-colored skin was spectacular.

"Babe."

Sophie swiped at the saliva gathering at the corner of her mouth as she stood inside the door of In the Shadows Ink.

"Babe."

She tore her eyes away from the tall, reserved man and met Zak's amused eyes.

"Should I be jealous?"

"Hell yes," she answered slowly.

He turned his lips in, biting them, fighting back a laugh. At least he wasn't angry about it.

Finally, he said, "Point taken. Mental note: don't leave my woman alone with Crow. Ever."

"That would probably be for the best."

"Babe," he said, shaking his head and looking at the ground.

"He got an ol' lady?"

Zak's lips twitched. "Nope."

"How is he not taken yet?" she whispered, turning her face away from Crow so he couldn't hear her.

"Some men don't wanna be caught."

"But you did."

He lazily lifted a shoulder. "Wasn't plannin' on it. Just happened."

"You want this done?" Crow called out impatiently, squeezing out ink from bottles into small cap-like cups.

"He good at this?" Sophie asked Zak softly.

"I'm good," Crow grunted.

Whoops.

Zak wrapped an arm around her shoulder. "The best, babe."

"Brother, where do ya want this?" Crow asked as they moved closer to the tattoo chair.

"Want her over my heart, but Bear's there, so..."

SOPHIE WINCED as she studied the fresh ink that Zak now sported down his forearm in the limited space he had there. The large black script lettering that read *Sophie* was wrapped in plastic.

She gritted her teeth. No one told her this would be worse than getting a cavity filled. The whine of the tattoo gun was almost as bad as a dentist's drill.

She sighed in relief when Crow finally grunted, "Done," and put down that instrument of torture. Her skin felt like it was on fire.

"Fuck, babe," Zak murmured, checking it out and blocking her view.

"Is that a good 'fuck?'"

He turned his head to look at her, his eyes warm as he practically glowed with pride. "You know it is."

Crow wiped near her right hip with a damp paper towel that felt cool on her irritated skin.

"Let me see," she said impatiently to Crow, who lifted his beautiful head and gave her an equally impatient look with his intense black, but oh-so-beautiful eyes.

Damn. She might have to rethink this tattoo. Maybe get a few letters changed out...

"Babe." Zak's amused voice snapped her back to reality.

She bent forward and peered down at her hip, sucking in a breath.

The words "Property of Z" were now permanently marked in her skin.

It had been Bella's idea since Sophie didn't want to wear a cut, especially when trying to run a respectable business in town. When Zak had said he was going to get her name put on his body, she confessed her plan.

Her man had been speechless for a good five minutes. Then he fucked her good for a solid hour.

And as soon as he rolled off her, he had snagged his cell phone and dialed Crow to set up an appointment.

He wanted to make sure she didn't change her mind.

She didn't.

"Now we won't need wedding bands, right?" she teased.

He cocked an eyebrow. "We'll see."

She smiled. "Love you, baby."

"Love ya, babe."

"Fuckin' get outta here with that mushy shit," Crow barked, rolling his stool away, his face twisted up.

"Aw, Crow, one day you might be tattooing a woman's name on your own body," Sophie ribbed him.

"Never gonna happen," Crow answered, shaking his head, frowning.

"Never say never, brother," Zak said, laughing and whacking him on the back. "Get my woman wrapped up so I can take her home an' show her how much I like my mark on her."

At his words, Sophie smiled.

Sign up for Jeanne's newsletter to keep up with book news and upcoming releases:

http://www.jeannestjames.com/newslettersignup

Down & Dirty: Jag

Welcome to Shadow Valley where the Dirty Angels MC rules. Get ready to get Down & Dirty because this is Jag's story...

The only thing Jag, DAMC Road Captain, loves more than his custom bike is Ivy. He's wanted her ever since he could remember. However, through the years, he's had to watch her date anyone but him since she avoids dating bikers like the plague. Instead, she gravitates toward the complete opposite: geeks and nerds. Something Jag will never be.

Smart and independent, Ivy wants to be the property of no man. Growing up in the club, she knows firsthand how they treat women. She regrets the mistake she made by dragging Jag upstairs to his room at the club one drunken night. Ever since then, she's been doing her best to keep him at arm's length, though it's proven difficult. Especially when she finds out his secret, which only endears her to him even more.

Between secrets, lies, and a violent tangle with a rival club, can these two passionate hot-heads find the love and solace they're looking for in each other's arms? Or will everything just tumble down around them?

Turn the page to read the first chapter of book two in the Dirty Angels MC series:
Down & Dirty: Jag

Down & Dirty: Jag

Chapter One

He was going to kill the bitch.

Jag pounded on the door. Again.

She was pushing him to his limit. And that was not good.

For him.

For her.

For the human race in general.

"Fuckin' open the door or I'll bust the fuckin' thing in, got me?"

He was going to knock politely only one more time, then that was it.

He *politely* kicked the door with his heavy biker boot. That was going to leave a mark.

"If you don't open this fuckin' door right—"

The door jerked open and something—or someone—tried to fly by him.

Jag reached out a hand and snagged the fleeing body. With a grip around a skinny bicep, the guy came to a screeching halt.

Jag flung him around to face him. He scowled. "Who the fuck are you?"

The already pale guy turned sheet white. With eyes wide, mouth open, he had a discarded shirt bunched in his fist and his pants hung loosely around his hips, since he apparently hadn't taken the time to finish fastening them before the man decided to jet.

Which was a smart move. But then, Ivy tended to pick smart dudes. Though, they never hung around long. Geeky dudes and a biker babe don't mix no matter how many times she tried.

And he got it, he really did. Ivy was smart herself. Genius even. And she needed a challenge.

Other than becoming a biker's ol' lady. Or his ol' lady, more like it.

Jag looked down at the guy's bare feet. It seemed he forgot his fucking shoes in his haste.

Stupid fuck. Maybe he wasn't so smart after all.

"You touch Dirty Angels' property?"

The guy's mouth opened and closed like a guppy as he stared up at Jag, who towered over him by at least five inches.

"Asked a damn question. Did you—"

"Get gone, Jag."

His eyes slid to the woman now standing in the doorway, holding out a pair of loafers with socks tucked into them. The one wearing a fucking *robe* and probably *nothing else*.

The guy's eyes dropped to his offered shoes, then he snagged them and clasped them to his chest as if they were a lifeline.

"Get in the house. Deal with you shortly."

"The hell you will. *Get gone*, Jag."

His head twisted in her direction and he took his time inspecting her from top to toe. That fucking deep red hair of hers spilled around her shoulders, clearly messed up from a fresh fuck, which he hoped he'd interrupted. Because if anyone should be in her bed, it should be him.

Her lips were swollen and pouty. Goddamn, if she had those lips around this nerd's cock, his brain would explode. Her green eyes snapped in anger.

Whatever. She could be mad all she wanted. He was just as pissed. No, more.

"Who I fuck is none of your damn business," came out of that smart mouth.

He gritted his teeth before answering. "The fuck it isn't. Anything to do with DAMC property is my business."

Especially after she climbed into his bed all those months ago.

"Well, I'm not DAMC property. So *GET GONE*!"

Jag released the now very scared guy with a shove. He stumbled, caught his balance on the veranda railing, then ran down the metal stairs, taking two at a time. Like a scared mouse, he sprinted toward a car parked on the street.

He should've known the guy drove a fucking Prius. He should've slashed the geek-mobile's tires for dipping his dick in DAMC property.

"Fucker doesn't even ride a bike. You've got shit taste in lays, Ivy."

"Don't I know it," she muttered, making Jag's jaw tighten.

"Don't come back here," Jag yelled his warning through the dark to the guy scrambling into his car like his ass was on fire. "If you know what's good for ya," he finished under his breath. He turned back to face the pissed-off redhead dressed in black silk that hugged all her damn curves. His balls tightened as hard as his jaw. "Probably needs a dick extension to fuck you."

"I don't know if that's an insult to me or to him. Either way, you don't belong here, Jag. So, I'll say it again, get gone."

"Not leavin'."

Ivy lifted a shoulder. "Okay then. You'll be standing out here all night while I'm sleeping soundly in my bed. Thanks to you, alone. Normally, I'd say good night, but... fuck you."

The door slammed shut and Jag heard the deadbolt click. He grimaced and stared at the door.

Little did she know that her uncle, Ace, had given him the key.

He grinned, turned on his heel and jogged down the steps to where his bike was parked at the foot of the stairway in the pawn shop lot.

She may not let him in, but his mission was accomplished. He chased away Ivy's latest conquest.

And he'd keep doing it until she got some sense and realized everything she needed had been right in front of her all along.

He put his girl between his legs, hit her starter and closed his eyes for a moment, surrounded by the smooth rumble of his straight exhaust pipes.

His bike was everything to him. The only thing he wanted more between his legs was Ivy.

The only thing he loved more than his bike was... *fucking* Ivy.

And she was a fucking bitch.

IVY LEANED her head back against the door, her hands covering her face as she tried not to scream. She sucked in a deep, shaky breath in an attempt to control her temper, as well as her frustration. She wasn't having much luck.

Fucking Jag.

Finally, she heard the roar of his bike before it faded away.

Coast was clear.

She had no idea how the brother knew she had a man in her apartment. It was like he had some sixth sense. This wasn't the first time he'd chased a man away.

Probably wouldn't be the last.

The problem with being raised in a motorcycle club and being around bikers her whole life was just that... being around a bunch of misogynistic macho bikers.

Women were considered property of the club. *Property*. And being born into a bloodline of bikers made it hard to escape that.

Not that she necessarily wanted to escape. She loved her brothers and she loved her life for the most part.

She did well financially working in her uncle's pawn shop and living above it rent-free. She also had gone to school for computers and programming, so she ran the club's website, all the club's businesses' websites and fixed any of the club member's computers when needed. In all reality, she could open her own computer shop if she wanted. She knew how to diagnose, knew how to program.

The club relied on her a lot. Sometimes she even helped Ace, the club's Treasurer, run the numbers for the club's finances.

She was smart. But sometimes she just did dumb things.

Like sleeping with Jag once during a drunken mistake one night after a pig roast. She had lost her mind and dragged him upstairs to his room at the clubhouse. Ever since then, there'd been tension between them.

Luckily, Ace never found out because, even though the man was her uncle, he acted like a father to her, especially since she never knew her real father. And though he loved Jag like a son, she wouldn't put it past him to kick the younger man's ass for "defiling" Ivy.

Even though Jag was in no way her first lover.

Ace tended to encourage Ivy to date men outside the club. Though she wasn't sure why since he was an engrained member of the club himself. So, he couldn't think the brothers weren't good enough. Could he?

Maybe he was just overprotective.

Who knew.

But Ivy slipped up that night, Jag didn't fight it and now she'd regretted it ever since.

Because the last thing she wanted was to be wearing a "Property of Jag" vest similar to the cuts that some of the other ol' ladies wore.

She was an independent woman, goddamn it, and intended on staying that way come hell or high water.

But she had to admit that the guy she had brought home tonight wasn't for her. He was just going to scratch an itch. The "date" they went on had been boring. He was a nice guy, sure, and cute enough. However, the spark was missing.

Both her and Jag had been drunk as all get out when they hooked up. That night there weren't sparks either. No, there had been explosions.

And that scared her to death.

JAG SAT at the large lacquered wood table. The one that had the Dirty Angels MC logo carved in it all those years ago by one of the founding members, his granddaddy Bear.

May the brother rest in peace.

The way things were going, it didn't seem that there would ever be peace. Ever since Bear was killed by a Shadow Warrior back in the eighties, things had been a little rocky.

Which brought his thoughts to his father, Rocky, who was serving a life sentence at SCI Greene for taking out a few of those Warriors in retribution.

But even after all these years, the bad blood between the two clubs hadn't lessened. The Warriors showed up now and again to create havoc like a bad fucking penny.

And now because of recent events, the club prez, Pierce, was sitting at the head of the table talking about keeping security beefed up at all the club's businesses. Which put a bigger strain on Diesel, who was both the club's enforcer and in charge of In the Shadows Security, which provided bouncers to area bars as well as personal and commercial security to those who could afford it.

"Need to keep vigilant." Pierce glanced around the table, his eyes bouncing from one executive member to the next. "Even the ol' ladies, so spread the word to them, too. Fucker had a set on him when he tried to snag Sophie right in front of Z on a busy street. If she'd been by herself, no tellin' what woulda happened to her."

Head nods and pounding of fists went around the table.

"Can tell you what would happen if they took one of our ol' ladies, a fuckin' slaughter, that's what," Diesel grumbled.

"No doubt," Hawk agreed.

"Yeah, an' then we all end up at Greene in adjoinin' cells like Rocky and Doc," Ace, the oldest member and the coolest head in the room said to both of his sons.

Jag whacked him on the arm. "Then, brother, you and me both would get to see our pops."

Ace frowned. "Ain't funny, boy."

"Respect to Doc and Rocky," Dex shouted, causing a few hoots and hollers.

Pierce pounded the gavel on the table. "Okay, okay. Settle down so we can get through our business an' I can go bust a nut in my woman."

They all chuckled.

"Now, anybody got shit goin' down with the Dark Knights?" Pierce pinned his gaze on the large man at the other end of the table. "Diesel?"

"Nothin' new."

He looked to his left. "Hawk?"

"Only thing I got wind of is they took over Dirty Dick's Bar."

Pierce frowned. "Took over?"

Hawk leaned forward to look down the table at Pierce. "Not runnin' it. At least not yet. Mostly usin' it as a regular hangout for anyone wearin' their colors."

"That's just south of the city line." Which could be concerning since it was farther out of the city than they've been before.

"Yup."

"They pushin' shit?"

Hawk raised a brow. That was enough of an answer for Pierce. He muttered, "Shit."

Dex spoke up. "Last thing we need is them runnin' drugs or guns through Shadow Valley. Don't want 'em stirrin' up the local boys in blue."

"That's for fuckin' sure," Jag muttered. "Bad enough Axel's always hangin' 'round Sophie's bakery."

"That's 'cause he's sniffin' 'round Bella," Ace volunteered with a frown.

"I'll kill the fucker," Diesel said. The club's Sergeant at Arms was a bit overly protective of his cousin. Though, for good reason.

Ace looked at his younger son. "You ain't doin' shit, boy."

"We can just hurt 'im a bit," Hawk added.

Ace's head swung to his oldest and he pointed a finger toward him in warning. "You neither, boy. Leave him be. It'll sort sooner than later. You know better than to fuck with SVPD."

"But if they're fuckin' with DAMC—"

Pierce jumped in. "Let it go for now. Got enough other shit goin' on than Axel gettin' a boner over Bella."

Diesel's body visibly tightened and his face twisted into a scowl. Hawk crossed his beefy arms over his chest and sat back in his chair, clearly unhappy with the order.

Though no matter what their father or their president said, the brothers would always step in to protect their cousin. No question about it.

And because of that, Jag knew he had to be careful with what could happen between him and Ivy, Bella's sister. She wasn't quite on their radar like Bella was, but it wouldn't take but a misstep to put her there. And he didn't need a hassle from either of them.

Jag might not be a small man and he made sure to keep in shape, but those two could pound him into the ground before he could say "boo." Best to stay on their good side.

Pierce leaned back in his chair. "Maybe it's time for a sit-down with the Knights. See if they're willin' to clue us in on what their intentions are. We don't wanna be caught with our panties down 'round our ankles."

"That's for damn sure," Dex said.

Ace nodded. "Agreed."

"All in favor?" Pierce asked.

"Ayes," rose up around the table.

"If they're not willing to chit chat, maybe we can get someone on the inside. One of Dawg's girls or somethin'," Dex suggested. "Just a thought."

"Not sure if the Knights will easily accept an obvious stripper into their fold. But you never know," Pierce said. "Pick a bitch that ain't so obvious. But they might agree to a sit-down, we can go that route first."

Dex continued, "If we need a plant, it's gotta be one loyal to the club. No doubt. We ain't takin' them down, we're just tryin' to get a little info on their territory grab. But still need to send in snatch that ain't gonna run her damn mouth. Not sure if we can trust one of Dawg's girls for that."

"Should we even ask for a sit-down first? Might give 'em a head's up. Maybe send in a bitch, get some info, *then* ask for a sit-down once she's clear," Diesel suggested.

Pierce turned toward Diesel. "Handle it. Talk to Dawg, see if any of his girls are reliable enough. If not, we may have to approach this from a different angle."

"Got it," Diesel grunted.

"All right, enough of the fuckin' bad news. This is a fuckin' MC an' we haven't had a group ride in a while so we need to get on that." Pierce looked pointedly at Jag. "Yo Road Captain, make it happen for Saturday. Got me?"

Jag nodded in agreement. "Gotcha. Certainly could use it. 'Specially now the weather turned."

A couple "yeahs" rose from the other members of the Executive Committee.

"Good. See it done. Hawk, plan a roast for after. Get the bitches to put somethin' together. An' get Mama Bear in the kitchen to make some good grub to go along with the hog."

"Done," Hawk grumbled, clearly still stewing about Bella and Axel.

Jag might have to give his cousin a head's up. Axel may be a cop, but he was still blood.

"We done here?" Pierce asked, looking around the table. When no one spoke up, he said, "Good," and pounded the gavel on the table.

As everyone pushed back their chairs and filed out, Ace put a hand on Jag's arm and tilted his head indicating for him to hold back.

Fuck.

Ace waited until the last member left the meeting room, then turned his attention to Jag. "Brother, you're like a son to me, but we need to have a sit-down of our own."

"'Bout what?" Jag asked, but he knew.

He definitely knew.

Ivy probably ran her mouth to her uncle first thing this morning at the pawn shop.

"You showin' up in the middle of the night at the apartment."

"Wasn't the middle of the night."

Ace just gave him a look.

Jag shrugged and repeated, "Wasn't."

"No matter. You got her all jacked up this morning. Had to hear her bitchin' for twenty minutes straight. What's goin' on between you two?"

"Nothin'."

"Well, I know that's bull. No reason for you to make yourself known every time she's got some man in her place."

There were plenty of reasons, just none he wanted to spill. "That don't bother you?"

"Not my business."

Right. But if it was one of the brothers doing nightly visits to Ivy's bed, Jag just bet Ace would make it his business. "I'm just lookin' out for her like Hawk an' D do for Bella. Bein' protective."

Ace snorted and shook his head. "Right."

"Somebody's gotta protect our women."

"You know Dex is perfectly fine with watchin' out for his sisters when it comes to that."

"Dex don't care who's crawlin' in an' out of their beds."

"Then maybe you shouldn't either."

Damn.

Ace continued. "What's your end game? 'Cause you know I don't want her endin' up with a brother. Sure as shit don't want her endin' up like Bella did."

Jag blinked. "That shit'll never happen again. An' it definitely wouldn't happen with me."

"So, you got interest," Ace stated rather than asked.

Fuck. He fell right into that trap.

Nothing like looking a man he respected in the eye and telling him that he's interested in fucking his niece, who was like a daughter to him. Ace might be in his fifties but he sired Hawk and Diesel, two very big guys. And the man was no slouch himself. Plus, he didn't need bad blood between them, anyway.

"You got no problem with her apartment havin' a revolvin' door?"

That may have been the wrong thing to say. Ace's eyes narrowed and his shoulders squared off.

Fuck.

"You sayin' she's as bad as a sweet butt?"

Holy fuck. She better not be as bad as one of the sweet butts, the eager women who hung around church to service any of the brothers whenever and wherever they wanted it. Most of them did it in hopes of one day becoming an ol' lady. Which, for most, would never happen. Brothers didn't want to make a sweet butt an ol' lady. Nobody wanted something permanent with what everyone else may have had.

"Not sayin' that."

"Good. But maybe the door would stop revolvin' if you stopped chasin' every guy she dates away."

Dates. *Right.*

Ace continued, "Makes me think you're hung up on her, Jag. Makes me wonder if I should take that key back I gave you for an emergency."

"Haven't abused that key. Always knock."

"Yeah, probably have to paint the door to cover up that *knock* from last night."

"You need it painted, I'll get it done."

Ace lifted his chin. "Yeah, I'll let you know if the mark don't come off. Then your ass can fix your fuck up."

Next time, he'd just use the key when Ivy refuses to open the door. That would really get her going.

"She gotta gun?"

Ace's eyebrows rose. "Why?"

"Just askin'."

"So, you plannin' on interruptin' her next time she's got a date?"

"Yep."

Ace dropped his head and shook it. His shoulders moved with what looked like laughter. "Fuck, boy. You're lucky I like you."

Jag smiled. "Know it, Ace. Promise I won't ever hurt her."

"Better not. 'Cause I'll kick your ass myself. An' I'll kick it if you repeat this, but somebody's got to tame her wayward ways. She's restless. She ain't findin' what she's lookin' for. That's obvious by that 'revolving door' you mentioned. Maybe it's high time a brother tried to get her to settle down."

"So, I got your blessin'?" Jag asked, surprised at this sudden turn.

"Didn't say that. An' it all ain't up to me." Ace studied him for a moment with his lips pursed and his hands on his hips, making Jag shuffle his feet uncomfortably. "You know she don't do bikers. That's gonna be a hurdle right there."

Little did he know she already had done one. Once. "Just needs to do one."

Ace shook his head. "Right. If she don't want you, you gotta drop this shit, hear me? An' then let her figure out what she wants on her own."

"Hear ya. Won't be a problem."

"Just want her to be happy."

"You ain't the only one," Jag murmured.

"She'd have my nuts in a vise if she knew what we were talkin' about."

"No doubt. Don't think that nerd last night had any nuts though."

Ace snorted and slapped him on the back as they walked out of the meeting room into the common area of the clubhouse. "Surprised there wasn't a line of shit from the balcony all the way out to his car."

Jag grinned. "Yeah. Wouldn't be surprised at all if he shit his pants."

Get *Down & Dirty: Jag* here:
mybook.to/DAMC-Jag

If You Enjoyed This Book

Thank you for reading Down & Dirty: Zak. If you enjoyed Zak and Sophie's story, please consider leaving a review at your favorite retailer and/or Goodreads to let other readers know. Reviews are always appreciated and just a few words can help an independent author like me tremendously!

Bear's Family Tree

- **BEAR Jamison**
  DAMC Founder
  - **MITCH Jamison**
    Blue Avengers MC
    - **ZAK Jamison**
      DAMC (President)
    - **AXEL Jamison**
      Blue Avengers MC
    - **JAYDE Jamison**
  - **ROCKY Jamison**
    DAMC
    - **JEWEL Jamison**
    - **DIAMOND Jamison**
    - **JAG Jamison**
      DAMC (Road Captain)

Doc's Family Tree

		DIESEL Dougherty DAMC (Enforcer)
	ACE Dougherty DAMC (Treasurer)	
		HAWK Dougherty DAMC (Vice President)
		DEX Dougherty DAMC (Secretary)
DOC Dougherty DAMC Founder		
	ALLIE Dougherty	**IVY Doughtery**
		ISABELLA McBride
	ANNIE Dougherty	**KELSEA Dougherty**

Also by Jeanne St. James

Find my complete reading order here:

https://www.jeannestjames.com/reading-order

Standalone Books:

Made Maleen: A Modern Twist on a Fairy Tale

Damaged

Rip Cord: The Complete Trilogy

Everything About You (A Second Chance Gay Romance)

Reigniting Chase (An M/M Standalone)

Brothers in Blue Series

A four-book series based around three brothers who are small-town cops and former Marines

The Dare Ménage Series

A six-book MMF, interracial ménage series

The Obsessed Novellas

A collection of five standalone BDSM novellas

Down & Dirty: Dirty Angels MC®

A ten-book motorcycle club series

Guts & Glory: In the Shadows Security

A six-book former special forces series

(A spin-off of the Dirty Angels MC)

Blood & Bones: Blood Fury MC®

A twelve-book motorcycle club series

Motorcycle Club Crossovers:

Crossing the Line: A DAMC/Blue Avengers MC Crossover

Magnum: A Dark Knights MC/Dirty Angels MC Crossover

Crash: A Dirty Angels MC/Blood Fury MC Crossover

Beyond the Badge: Blue Avengers MC™

A six-book law enforcement/motorcycle club series

COMING SOON!

Double D Ranch (An MMF Ménage Series)

Dirty Angels MC®: The Next Generation

WRITING AS J.J. MASTERS:

The Royal Alpha Series

A five-book gay mpreg shifter series

About the Author

JEANNE ST. JAMES is a USA Today and international bestselling romance author who loves an alpha male (or two). She writes steamy contemporary M/F and M/M romance, as well as M/M/F ménages, and has published over 63 books (so far) in five languages. She also writes M/M paranormal romance under the name: J.J. Masters.

Want to read a sample of her work? Download a sampler book here: BookHip.com/MTQQKK

To keep up with her busy release schedule check her website at www.-jeannestjames.com or sign up for her newsletter: http://www.jeannestjames.com/newslettersignup

www.jeannestjames.com
jeanne@jeannestjames.com

Newsletter: http://www.jeannestjames.com/newslettersignup
Jeanne's Down & Dirty Book Crew: https://www.facebook.com/groups/JeannesReviewCrew/
TikTok: https://www.tiktok.com/@jeannestjames

facebook.com/JeanneStJamesAuthor
amazon.com/author/jeannestjames
instagram.com/JeanneStJames
bookbub.com/authors/jeanne-st-james
goodreads.com/JeanneStJames
pinterest.com/JeanneStJames

Get a FREE Sampler Book

This book contains the first chapter of a variety of my books. This will give you a taste of the type of books I write and if you enjoy the first chapter, I hope you'll be interested in reading the rest of the book.

Each book I list in the sampler will include the description of the book, the genre, and the first chapter, along with links to find out more. I hope you find a book you will enjoy curling up with!

Get it here: BookHip.com/MTQQKK

Printed in the USA
CPSIA information can be obtained
at www.ICGtesting.com
LVHW072144170923
758470LV00033B/291

9 781954 684676